Sealed With A Kiss

By K.N Marie

We will be donating $1 from every book sold to the #BringTeaghanHome foundation.

Teaghan was abducted in July 2021 and taken overseas by her grandparents. Her family has been fighting every day to bring her home. All over the world children are abducted by family members and their families spend years searching and fighting to bring them back home. We are stronger together.

I would like to dedicate this book to my younger brother, Xander. He died too young, and I want his memory to live on, in our hearts as well as others.

I would like to dedicate this book to my children Payton and Draven, always go after your dreams like I have mine.

Prologue:

Xander

As the older brother, it's my job to protect my sister, even if I'm only two years older. It became my sole responsibility the day our father died. He never told anyone he was sick; he hid it from us so that we wouldn't see him as a burden or treat him differently. He even wrote me, Olivia, and our mother a letter to explain why he did what he did. He told us that he wanted to enjoy every day of his life with us no matter what happened. Olivia used to have the typical girl dream; extravagant wedding, perfect husband, great job, you name it. She dreamed BIG! Then one day that all changed, that was the day that Tristan left her. I never had a good feeling about that man, correction, boy, only true men deserve to be called men. Men that actually grow up and don't abuse women. Sometimes I think that the only reason Olivia ever stayed with him was because dad told her to give him a chance, but why? Did he see something in him that we couldn't?

Olivia decided to say yes to his proposal and when they went to tell his parents they were not accepting, so he left her. I was so mad that day I saw my sister sitting outside her old apartment crying. She had forgotten her key and texted me to ask if I could swing by and let her in.

Seeing her sitting there in tears, was one of the worst days of my life. I brought her inside and made her tell me what had happened. She made me promise that I would never do anything to harm Tristan because "he wasn't worth it." I kept my word, but that won't stop me from stepping in when she finds another guy, the next guy to do this to her will pay.

My dearest Xander,

If you're reading this it means the time has come, I was hoping I would have longer with you all, but I knew this day was coming. I know it will come as a surprise, but I kept it from all of you so that you would never treat our time differently. You may feel hurt, that is normal, but just know that every day I got to spend with the three of you were the best days of my life. When I found out I was sick I tried to live every day to the fullest. If you or your sister wanted to do something with me, I made it happen.

You are the sole man of the house now, and with that comes great responsibility. I am not asking you to oversee anything, I just want you to look out for our girls. They are yours now and I leave them in your capable hands. Your mother will be distraught that I'm gone, as I would expect her to be and so will you and your sister. Just be strong for one another, that's all you can do. You will get through this.

Inside I've included some pictures of the happiest moments with each of you, I tried to capture as many as I could so that you wouldn't be left without pictures.

When my parents died, I didn't have any pictures of them and I didn't want it to be the same for you, it helps the healing process when you are able to look at them instead of hiding out in your head.

Now, make sure that your sister doesn't collapse in on herself, you know how she likes to hide sometimes. Protect her against men, there will be some frogs out there for her to kiss, this is normal. You may be asking why I say this when she is with Tristan, I don't expect her to stay with him, but I do think this is going to be a great steppingstone for her. You will go through the same thing my son, I have raised you to be a great man, respectful, responsible, everything a woman is looking for.

So do me a favour and just be yourself.

Remember to always be kind, even if someone hurts you, you know better than to attack them. Be the bigger person in life and it will get you far! I'm sorry that I didn't get to see you meet the girl of your dreams or your wedding, but just know I will always be there for you even if you can't see me.

I love you my son,
-Dad

I read the note my dad left me often, usually when my mom or Olivia are having a hard time, it reminds me of what he would have done or wanted me to do. He was a great father, best anyone could ever ask for. The pictures he left me made me smile and I hung them on my wall so that I could see them every day I came home. I don't want to forget about him, but I also do not want to live in the past, that's not healthy for anyone.

I'm waiting for Olivia to meet the next guy she thinks is the one so that I can give him my "you hurt her and you're dealing with me" speech.

Chapter One:

Olivia

When I was little, I use to dream of the perfect wedding with the perfect man. The perfect kiss, house, everything that came with it really. My parents had the perfect marriage so I always thought I would as well. Well let me tell you, that phrase "you need to kiss a couple frogs before you find your prince." It's not a joke people! That's the real deal right there. Now I'm sure we've all been there before, right? I mean who can say they found their soul mate in their first kiss?

Go ahead, I'll wait!

No one? I didn't think so, it is very far in between that happening. It's like winning the lottery, you have a one in a million chance. Usually, you don't win. So, you try again, and again, and again.
Well, that was always my motto: try, try again until you find the one. So, I had my childhood crush of course, you know the one I'm talking about. The first boy you start to actually get feelings for when you're little. Yeah, that one, turns out he thought I had cooties, so that did not

work out. It is how I met my best friend Marina though, but more on her later.

When I got to grade six, I had another crush, he turned out to be a bully to my brother. I won't stand for that sort of thing, so that ended quickly as well. In grade nine I developed a new crush, we dated for a few months, but nothing serious ever happened, he was my first kiss though. But then he found another girl he liked more and that was the end of that. At this point in my life my mom was starting to learn that she had to help pick up the pieces of what I thought was my broken heart, before my brother got to them. We started a tradition where we would go shopping, get some ice cream and watch a bunch of movies that made us cry. That way we could say we were crying from the movies instead of a broken heart. Men do not deserve the opportunity to say they broke your heart. Remember that ladies, if you only take one piece of advice from me, take that.

We didn't need Xander going and knocking everyone out, because then he would never get anywhere in life. So eventually we stopped telling him and just went about our business. A lot of boys hurt me growing up, but I like to look at it as helping me mature into the woman I am today.

When I got into high school, I tried dating again, but at this point who am I kidding, everyone was a dick head and just wanted to get laid. Not that anyone was old enough at this point, but experimenting you know…

Later, I started to give up on finding the right one, because let's be honest, only a few find their one in school. How they did I have no idea, but good on them. I went on a couple dates here and there after high school, but nothing ever came of them until one day my dad decided to set me up with one of his friend's sons, Tristan. He was good looking, and I figured it would make my dad happy to give him a chance, so I did. We went on a few dates and then he started to show his true colours and I didn't like it. But I stuck with him because I figured I was being dramatic. Needless to say, that didn't work out and now here we are, where my story begins. At this point in my life, I meet men at bars, go to their house, fuck, leave a note, and never see them again. It's a way to protect myself, I'm not proud of it but it works for me. So why mess with something that works?

Chapter Two:

Damon

I sit here staring at my computer screen, cursing my mother for making my brother and I identical twins. Technically it is not her fault, but she made it happen, so I'm saying it is. Many people don't know that we are, they think I'm the player the internet has made me out to be. But that's my brother, Erik, I do tend to be seen with women occasionally, a man has needs. I have the need to feel a warm pussy wrapped around my cock. All men do. If they say otherwise, they are lying.

However, most of the time I am seen with a woman it is because I needed a date to go to a function I was attending. I am typically seen with my friend and reporter Mia; she helps keep my face out of the news. My brother and I are a hot commodity, so we make the news all the time. My brother and I may look alike, with our dark hair and blue eyes, but that doesn't mean we are the same. I like to think of myself as a kind-hearted male that respects women whereas my brother just sees women as something to fuck. He gets us put in the news for being with women, whereas I get us in the news for the company-based things.

I stare at the newest pictures circulating the web, my brother with his hand on some woman's backside going into a restaurant, followed by a hand on her tit in the middle of supper. Why does he do this to us? It wouldn't be so bad if the internet would mention that it wasn't me, but after college I decided not to tell people I was a twin anymore. The only way you would be able to tell is if you looked for the dimple on Erik's face when he's smiling. Both a good and bad thing, everyone uses my name in the tabloids therefor I get pegged as a playboy. We both own the business, we both look the same, but we do not act the same.

Not many people know there's two of us, yet the company is named Thomson and Thomson. I mean unless it was my father and I working together, I don't see how someone couldn't put two and two together. If someone asks if I have a brother I won't lie to them, I just don't go out of my way to say I do. Like I said, it's not how you sell magazines to the public with blind eyes. It's not that I'm embarrassed of my brother, I just don't need a repeat of college if I can avoid it. Mia was willing to help me, but I had to give her something to work with as well.

Mia

I'm sorry to cancel on you at the last minute but I'm not feeling well so I won't be able to make it tonight.

Damon
*No problem, health is important. I hope you feel
better soon. I'll have some soup sent over
tomorrow.*

                                        Mia
*You're to good to me, thank you! I hope you
have a good night.*

Tonight, I am being forced to go to an event for
some restaurant foundation fundraiser. All I
know is that it's for charity, other than that I know
nothing, I'm not very interested in going. It could
be that my usual date for things like this had to
cancel on me last minute, so I must go solo.
Usually, I would take Mia to the event, we stay
for a few hours and then go back to my place,
fuck and go our separate ways. I would like to
say that I made this rule, but that would be a lie,
she did. She agrees to go with me to these
events as long as I get her off. She is a local
reporter, because of that our photos never
ended up in the local tabloids, unlike my brother.
I wish I added that part into our agreement. We
had met at a gala when we launched Thompson
and Thompson, her, Erik, and me got a photo
together there. It is probably the only one that
went public with both Erik and I together. Mia
had made quite the impression on me. She was
career driven and made it clear that she had no
time for relationships. I could respect that,
although she is a pretty girl, I didn't see a future
with her.

My phone starts ringing just as I do up my last cuff link, it's my assistant Stacy. "Good evening."

"Good evening Mr. Thomson, I wanted to let you know that your car is 5 minutes away."

"Thank you, Stacy, is that all?"

"Yes sir."

"I'm wondering if you can set up to have a bouquet of flowers, soup and a sandwich sent to Mia tomorrow for lunch please. She is not feeling well and can't make it tonight."

"Oh! That's not good. I will do that as soon as were off the phone. Do you want me to contact someone else and get them to meet you at the event? Or I can quickly get ready and meet you there myself."

"No need, thank you though. I can handle this one solo. Good night, I will see you in the office on Monday. Feel free to send yourself something for lunch tomorrow as well." Stacy had never offered to do that before, not only would it not be appropriate, but it would be very awkward.

"Thank you, sir, I'll see you on Monday."

Stacy is my new assistant after Dorothy retired. She picked up quickly and has been doing fantastic for only being with me a couple months. She is constantly running around but always at her desk when I need her.

We hang up and I make my way to the door after one last look in the mirror. I pet my husky Jack on the head and let him know I'll be home later; he looks up at me and wags his tail. I look sharp tonight, top of the line black suit with a baby blue dress shirt, black pants and shoes. I should be the poster child for tall, dark and handsome, I'm 6'4, have dark hair and bright blue eyes. I've worked hard on my physique as well; I try to run with my dog Jack at least three times a week. Jack is a black and white husky with a small patch of brown on his chest, I've had him since he was a pup. Every other day we take a walk in the morning before work. I go to the gym downstairs once or twice a week as well. I don't want to be bulky, but I want to have muscle and be a treat to look at, I think I accomplish that with my six pack, I haven't had any complaints. I think it is safe to say that if I really wanted to, I could have pretty much any woman. But I don't particularly like sleeping around, so I'll leave that to my brother.

I make my way downstairs to the waiting car, say hello to the driver, Henry, and get in. I never saw the point in renting out a limo for one person, but I am told I'm too much of a billionaire not to. At this point I just do what I am told, I would be perfectly fine driving myself or arriving in a town car.

My brother isn't allowed to go to events anymore, the last time he did one of the volunteers was found in the bathroom with his cock down her throat. It would not have been a problem if someone hadn't walked in on them, say like the planner themselves. Or if they would have at least been in a stall, but no, right out there in the open. I had to pay a lot of money to make it so that didn't make the front page of the newspaper the next day.

I arrive at the hotel the event is being held at and am surprised to see that they have gone all out. They have waiters walking around taking drink orders and handing out champagne. There are also women circulating with different hors d'oeuvre, which I'm assuming are smaller versions of things they sell at their restaurants. Honestly, I cannot wait to have some dessert, I love a good piece of cake.

Chapter Three:

Olivia

Tonight, is the night of the auction, I've been planning this event for months and now it's finally going to happen. This is in support of a charity dear to everyone's heart, every couple months we do a charity event to help out a different cause, this month it is for the children's hospital. I don't pick the charities, someone higher above me does, but who doesn't want to help kids, right? We have everything anyone would ever expect from an event being held by a restaurant franchise, servers going around with different samples of things we serve at our locations, endless supply of alcoholic and non-alcoholic beverages and let's not forget the dessert buffet. The main event of the evening is the auction that I somehow got roped into being part of. You see, I had suggested we do an auction for a date with a woman, and the higher ups thought it was an amazing idea. However, that meant that I was roped into being one of the ladies being auctioned off for a date. I got one of my best friends, Chellsea, as well seeing as she is one of the only single women I know. She is a hopeless romantic and also works for the company, so it was perfect. Chellsea was so excited when I told her that I volunteered her because she thinks she will find her Prince Charming. I gave up on that band wagon a long time ago and now I just have one-night stands, hoping to sneak out before they get up and make things awkward. You're probably wondering what made me this way. Well, let me tell you. I used to be with this man, Tristan. Our dads had set us up, things were rocky at first but after my dad passed, I clung onto him, and things were okay until he proposed. Long story short his parents didn't see me as long-term wife material. This doesn't stop him from trying to sleep with me every time he sees me, ugh I hate men like that. Now I just stick to sleeping with men, us both getting off, and then moving on. I mean, come on, a woman has needs.

I was nervous about the event to say the least, this is the first one that I have been in charge of. My girls were in the living room waiting on me. We all share a duplex together; Aly had renovated it so that there is a door that attaches the two houses together.

"Are you ready to go, you sexy bitch? The cars going to be here any minute!" Marina says to me while I finish touching up my mascara in our shared bathroom.

"Yes, just touching up my makeup, be out in a second."

Tonight, I am wearing a red dress with my signature red lipstick. It's one of those dresses that have no back but is covered in the front. I have my blonde hair down in loose waves and my blue eyes are popping out with the Smokey eye I have created for tonight's look. I know this is a work function but that does not mean there's only going to be people I work with there, so if I can get lucky, I'm going to.

I walk out of the bathroom to find my friends sitting in the living room with a glass of wine in their hands. Marina slips me one as well and we all cheers for the night ahead in hopes that it will make the charity a lot of money. I slip on my black shoes so that I am ready when the car arrives, should be any minute.

"Oh, I can't wait to see who bids for me. Do you think there'll be a lot of eligible men there tonight?" Chellsea says, hardly managing to sit still she's so excited.

Marina pipes up "I don't care, I'm going for the food and booze. You know me, I live to party when I don't need to work." Marina was a bartender at a nearby pub, so usually she was working while others partied.

"There will definitely be a tonne of food and booze, and I guarantee you there will be lots of men as well. However, they don't know there is an auction for a date. They just think that it's a normal charity event where they come and spend money and then go home." I say as I see the car pull up "Oh, the car is here girls, let's go!" We quickly finished our glasses and headed out. My company was nice enough to send a town car as a thank you for all my hard work, but to be honest a bottle of wine would have been fine.

The only thing we need to worry about now is how to get home at the end of the night.

The event is going perfectly, just how I imagined it would. Everyone seems to be enjoying themselves and the food. We are gearing up for the main draw of the evening, the auction. My boss just informed me that we will be starting in ten minutes, so I am going around trying to find all the ladies that are participating.

I can't help noticing how many attractive men are here tonight, Chellsea is going to be happy with any of them, I think. There is one I noticed specifically: tall, dark, and handsome. He also has the brightest blue eyes I have ever seen; they make you want to get lost in them and never look for a way out. I tried to ask a co-worker if they knew who he was, and they said they thought his name was Erik Thompson. So of course, I quickly googled him and found out he's a player, ugh, of course he is. That goes with what I'm into right now though, maybe he'll bid for me; and then we can hook up and never see each other again. That is one nice thing about being with a player, they don't want anything else from you either, just sex. I tend to try and go to their house that way I can leave my note and be on my way before the awkward morning after conversation happens.

My boss, Gloria, walks onto the stage, taps the microphone to make sure its working then starts her speech. "Hello everyone and thank you so much for joining us tonight for the restaurant marketing campaign to help different charities. Tonight, we are raising money for the children's hospital and getting our name out there as a business. We have 25 gorgeous women to auction off as dates. All proceeds will go to the children's hospital. Some of the women work for us and the others are our personal friends. We want to express that this is a date only and the bidding will begin at $500. I would like to introduce you to the beautiful bombshell of a woman that put this all together, Olivia Harper!" I walk onto the stage, give Gloria a hug and take the microphone from her "well thank you very much for that amazing introduction. I cannot thank you all enough for being here tonight to help us and the children's hospital. We have some amazing women here to auction off a date with themselves as well so let's get started. First up we have a feisty red head named Charlotte, she works in the office here as an assistant. She loves animals and walks on the beach. Do I have any takers?" Charlotte makes her way up onto the stage and does a little twirl, she looked so cute in her little black dress and tall as sin heels. "I would like to bid $500!" Said an attractive man with brown hair and green eyes.

"$1000!" "$1500" "$2000" said various men across the room.

A date with her sold for $2000 in the end which was a pretty good start in my opinion. The rest of the girls went for mostly the same, ranging from $1500-$3000.

"Second to last we have my best friend who is the sparkle in my eye on days I'm feeling low, she is an avid reader and a hopeless romantic, please welcome Chellsea to the stage." As I say this, I see her walk onto the stage blushing as she comes up and hugs me and then stands beside me scared that no one would bid for her, which is crazy because she is a brunette with killer looks, long legs and a nice ass to boot. "$1000" "$2000" "$2500" "$3000" she ends up going for $3500, I'm so happy for my friend! "Wow! You guys are doing amazing, so far, we have raised $52,000 do you think we can raise a little more? We only have one more girl to auction off a date with, can you guess who that might be? That's right, it's me! The bidding will once again start at $500, after this the dessert will be available and you will be able to talk to your dates and figure out where you'd like to take them. There is also a pay station by the front door so that you may make your donation for your date."

"$2500" I notice my ex; Tristan has joined the party to show off his chequebook. I'm not surprised he's bidding; he probably thinks it's an easy way to get into my pants. I tried to hide the disgust on my face.

"$4000" I hear Erik's voice before I see him raise his hand and shout out a number, wow that sure escalated quickly.

"$5000" I hear Tristen shout again.

"$8000" I see Xander spout out a number, knowing he won't win or can afford that I hope someone outbids him otherwise that would be fun to try and explain to people. Xander, is my older brother and it would look extremely funny if he won a date with me, so I'm hoping the bidding doesn't stop there. I know he's just trying to make me laugh by joining the bidding war going on over me.

"$10,000" Erik shouts again.

At this point I would be surprised if my mouth wasn't hanging open in shock like everyone else. No one has gone for this high and there's only two people bidding on me.

"$12,000" Tristen.

"$15,000" Erik.

"$17,000" Tristen.

"20,000" Erik.

"I'm out, you win!" Tristen shouts, walking away with a scowl on his face. Oh my god I am so happy that he did not win. That means I now have a date with the biggest player out there according to the internet. One that likes to also throw around his money, great! Can't wait!

"Okay, and that concludes that auction, I hope you all had fun. Now go enjoy the dessert and a few more drinks. Thank you all for coming and have a wonderful night! "I say into the microphone before turning it off and exiting the stage.

I go in search of my girls; I just know they are going to want to talk about what just happened. My phone goes off in my purse and I check it thinking it might be one of the girls telling me where they are, unfortunately I am left disappointed.

Tristan
You want to blow me in the coat closet? I'll make it worth your while.

Olivia
You're disgusting!

Tristan
Come on Livvy, it's not like we haven't done it before. One last roll in the hay. I know it's sort of your thing now.

I hate it when he calls me Livvy, I groan to myself and reply.

Olivia
Not with you it's not, you're the reason I started doing it. So how about you go away. Go use your hand for all I care!

Tristan
Come on baby you look so hot tonight; I would love to see those bright red lips wrapped around my cock. And then I would bend you over and fuck you with your dress around your waist and your heels on. Mmmmmmmmm, I can picture it now.

I decide to ignore his messages because they are already starting to put me in a bad mood, and I know that if I answer him, he will just keep texting back.

"Hey girl, we got you a glass of wine, that was a lot of work." Aly says.

I take it and take a sip "Ahhh, that tastes great. Thank you!"

Chapter Four:
Damon

I was not expecting there to be an auction tonight, but I am sure glad there was. When that blonde firecracker of a woman stepped up onto the stage and started auctioning off women, I was hoping that she would be a prize as well. She had the perfect body, long legs, long blonde hair, an ass that you just want to grab onto and a wonderful set of tits that you could see filled out her dress nicely. She picked a nice enough dress, I just think it could have been a little tighter, showed off her curves more, on the other hand though it leaves something for me to imagine. Because one way or another I'm taking her on a date, I want her in more ways than one.

There are 25 girls being auctioned off tonight it seems, we're on 24 right now, my chances of the last one being her are wearing thin. None of the other girls have interested me in the slightest because they are not her, I only have eyes for her. Number 24 is her best friend, so that leads me to believe that my chances are high, saving the best for last and all that.

My wish has come true, she is the last to be auctioned and she has the audacity to start herself off at $500, she is worth so much more than that. More than I could ever imagine putting a number on, I want to give her the world and I don't even know her yet.

"$2500" I hear from my left from a guy that looks like an asshole, or maybe I just hate him because he's bidding for what I want. Either way, that is still too low for what she's worth. I swore I saw her frown when she saw him, don't worry gorgeous he won't be going home with you.

"$4000" I shout and raise my arm, putting myself in on the bidding, by no means am I planning to end with this number I'm just curious to see how far this asshole is willing to go for her.

"$5000" he shouts back, turning to look at me and glare, silently telling me to back off. I don't think so bud, she's mine I give him a quick shake of my head.

"$8000" I hear a new voice shout from my right, when I turn to look at him, he's sitting with a group of girls and has a huge smile on his face. One of the girls swats him playfully telling him to sit down. Makes me wonder what's going on over there, I don't think he's a threat though.

"$10,000" I shout more aggressively than I probably needed to, but I want everyone to know that I was serious. I look back up onto the stage to catch another glimpse of my prize. I am imagining everywhere I could take her for our date, should I show off that I have money or that I'm down to earth? I think I'll go for the second one, seeing as she can clearly figure out, I have money, not that I peg her for a gold digger. I just like to treat my women well.

"$12,000" that asshole shouts again, I turn to look at him and shout back "$15,000". "$17,000" he shoots again, glaring at me now, begging me with his eyes for me to drop out so he can have her, well too bad bud, I want her more.

"$20,000" I hear a bunch of gasps around me as I turn to look at that guy that was bidding against me, I see his face crumble in defeat as he says, "I'm out, you win!" He scowls at me one last time and then storms out of the room. I look up at the beautiful woman I just won a date with to see her trying to hide her emotions, little does she know I am very good at reading people, that comes in handy in the bedroom.

Chapter Five:
Olivia

I walk over to where my girlfriends are all sitting and look at Xander "What in the hell were you thinking? What if they had stopped bidding and you were stuck paying $8000 for a date with me? We all know that you don't have the money for that. It would also look really funny if my BROTHER won a date with me, you do remember you're my BROTHER, right?" I added emphasis on the brother part to make sure it sunk in.

"Oh! Come on, you knew Tristen wouldn't give up that easy and then the way him and that guy were fighting over you, I knew I wouldn't end up having to pay. I just wanted to make it a little more interesting and up the cost of you a little more and hey it worked, didn't it? You're welcome! If anyone is 'winning' a date with my sister they better be willing to go all out, you deserve to have your world hung for you."

I scoff at him "what are you talking about? I don't even understand why Tristen is here or why he is bidding on me. He's the one that broke up with me remember? It never would have worked; his family is too involved in his decisions and I'm not good enough for them."

"That just means that you don't need to be in a relationship like that, girl. He was a douchbag to begin with and you're better off, I never liked him." Marina barks in to share her two cents.

"I know, I know, we've been over this before. Anyway, I should probably go find this guy that just paid $20,000 to go on a date with me. He better not be expecting me to open my legs because he donated to charity, that comes after a good date. I looked him up, he's a HUGE player!"

"You can't believe everything you see on the internet you know" Chellsea says, being the hopeless romantic, we all love.

"Don't worry if he's not the perfect gentleman then I'll have a talk with him! NO ONE hurts my baby sister and gets away with it." Xander says to me as he gets up, kisses my temple "I love you sis, you remember that."

He really is the best brother you could ask for, after my father died, he stepped up into the role of father as well. As far as I know no one ever asked him to, I think he just thinks that he's my protector, now that dad can't be.

***

I step into the bathroom and quickly touch up my makeup, and respray myself with perfume, I can't smell disgusting when I go meet this guy. Oh my god, he spent $20,000 to go on a date with me, that is ridiculous! Everyone else went for a maximum of $3500, there is no way I'm that attractive but okay, let's go meet this guy. When I come out of the bathroom, I notice that he is standing near the booth where you need to pay if you win, so that either means he's already paid or is waiting to.

I wander over to him and smile "Hi, my name is Olivia, and you won a very expensive date with me. Would you like to set up the details now or would you prefer to do it later though email or texting?"

"Hey, I'm Damon" he extends his hand out for me to shake, very professional. I put my hand in his and tried to hide my surprise when he kissed the back of my hand instead. If he is Damon, then who is Erik the internet is portraying him to be? Maybe Chellsea's right, you can't believe everything you read on the internet.

"Texting works for me, I'd rather just get to know you a little bit now if you're okay with that." He continued talking but I was already distracted. His mouth is sexy, the way he moves his lips when he talks makes me want to kiss him. Ugh, brain no stop it! He is not a piece of meat, I catch my eyes trailing down his body and stopping at his crotch, mmm how I'd like to see the package he's hiding under those pants "…. are you listening to me?" Damn, busted!

"Oh, um yea sorry I was, you said that texting would work for you and that you would like to get to know me a little bit tonight first."

A smile creeps upon his lips as he looks at me "I see you've missed the rest of it but that's okay, I get distracted looking at you too. Would you like to go grab a drink and we can exchange phone numbers?"

I nod, not allowing myself anymore speaking time at that moment afraid of what I might tell him. We go and grab a few desserts to snack on and a drink before sitting down to exchange numbers and make small talk. Would it be too forward of me to ask him to take me home tonight so that he can get me off and then we can just skip the date because then we would have already ended up getting what we really wanted? A nice easy hook up? Hmm... We will see how the night goes.

I know, I know, I just finished telling my brother and girlfriends that I would not spread my legs for him because he spent $20,000 on me, but I'm not one for relationships and I only want the one thing from him. Can't get hurt if it's just sex, that's what I always say!

"So, who came up with the idea for the auction? I've never been to a charity where the women are auctioned off before, usually it's the men" Damon says to me, I love the sound of his voice. "I did actually, I was playing around with the idea and mentioned it to the higher ups to raise more money and they went for it. Unfortunately, they said I needed to participate in order for it to go through. But that is a great idea, I will keep that in mind for future events." I winked.

He looks a little sad after that sentence "Well personally I can understand why they would want you to be part of it, you were the most attractive woman up there tonight. I am not trying to just get into your pants, I promise. I wasn't interested in the auction until you were auctioned off, then I just knew I had to win the date with you."

"You paid a lot of money just to have a date with me, why would you go through so much? Surely you don't need to pay women to go out with you." I say with a little grin on my face.

He lets out a small laugh "No, of course I don't. I like to donate to charity's though, I have more money than I know what to do with, so If I'm able to help someone in need I do. I also do a lot of charity work, I give a monthly allowance, if you will, to the food bank. I hate to see people starving when I can help, so I try. "

My heart melts a little at that "that is actually very sweet of you. Most people just keep money accumulating and then throw it around when they need to."

"You will notice that I'm nothing like normal rich men, I have a down to earth side."

I find it hard to believe that, but I will let him show me before I allow myself to judge him, or at least I'll try to.

We talk for roughly an hour about nothing in particular, I tell him what I do here, and he tells me what he does as a charity donator and potential investor in the company. Afterwards I go back to my girls for the rest of the night where we dance and drink way too much before going home. We are going to be feeling it in the morning for sure.

I wake up in the morning thankful that I do not need to go into work today. I walk out into the kitchen I see all the girls sitting there looking the way I feel.

"I made the coffee" says Chellsea, she's a little to chipper for someone that's supposed to be hungover like the rest of us. But she is probably running on the fact that she has a date with a potential contender to be her husband.

"Thank you" I say as I reach for my mug, fill it, and sit down to join the girls. "So, I'm assuming that since we're all here, none of us ended up getting lucky?"

Everyone shakes their head "no, but you looked mighty comfortable talking to Erik last night. I'm surprised you didn't end up going home with him." Marina says.

"I didn't want to come off as desperate, although I'm sure I could have told him I was interested in that, and we could have skipped the date. His name is Damon though, not Erik."

"Oh, I thought you said his name was Erik. Come on, you're not even the slightest bit excited to see where he's going to take you?" Chellsea looks at me with hope in her eyes. She does not fully understand why I do not want to date, just hook up.

"Yeah, the woman I overheard talking must have gotten his name confused because it's Damon. So, I am not sure how she got Erik, but oh well. And I'm excited to get a nice meal and hopefully get laid" I winked and took a sip of my coffee.

My comment was met with groans around the table.

"Come on Liv, really? Weren't you saying last night that you wouldn't spread your legs because of this?" Marina sighed. Apart from Chellsea, all my friends knew what I have gone through, they know why I only do one-night stands, but lately they have been pushing me towards domestication which is funny considering most of them are single.

"I'm going on the date isn't that enough? Normally I pick up guys at the bar they take me home and wham bam thank you madam we're done." I really do not feel like defending myself this morning.

"Well, whatever you do don't leave your note behind this time" Aly pointed her finger at me.

I rolled my eyes, the note has been an important piece to my adventures, it is the best way to leave, and no feelings get hurt. I do this because I do not do relationships but the last thing, I want to do is leave some poor sucker heartbroken after a night of amazing sex with me.

So, I always leave a note 'Thanks for the great night' and seal it with a kiss. No numbers, no second dates and most importantly no heart break.

"I'm not making promises that I can't keep, but I will consider it" I nursed my coffee to give me some relief from the hangover that is killing me this morning. My answer seemed to satisfy them enough to stop arguing. When I suggested we order some breakfast to be delivered the whole argument on my love life was forgotten and were focused on more important matters...our hangovers.

Chapter Six:
Damon

I stepped into the kitchen to find my brother Erik sitting at my island with two cups of coffee in his hand, a bag behind him and Jack laying in his bed "Hey, good morning brother. I thought I would stop in and see how last night went. Also, I took Jack out already." He hands me the cup; I take a sip as I sit down beside him.

"Thank you, it was good. There was an auction and I bid on a date with the most amazing girl, her name is Olivia, and she is the organizer, she put it all together."

"An auction? Like for girls?" He slaps his leg "of course they would make there be an auction when I'm not allowed to go to these things anymore, why couldn't they have done one when I was allowed to go?"

"It was an auction to go on a date with a girl, so it's not for sex."

"I know that I'm not an idiot. But usually if you take a girl out on a date, or a few, you can get in their pants. Therefor it is for sex as well, as long as you're smooth." He responds with a wink "I can give you some pointers if you'd like."

"I'm going to pretend that you don't see women as just objects that walk around for your pleasure."

"Oh, come on, you know I love the ladies. And I know they are not just for sex. Trust me, I don't have to pay for sex, usually they come to me, I just don't disappoint." He winks at me again. "As much as I would love to continue to talk about your dick all day, can we not? I also need you to stop winking at me, it's getting weird. Were you needing something, or did you just want to hang out? Also, what's in that bag? I'm starving."

He hands it over, I peak inside and see one chocolate croissant, I breathe it in and then take a big bite, these things will be the death of me. "Mmmmmmm, this is delicious, thanks again!" "Anytime, you know its tradition that if we're going to the other's house in the morning, we bring a coffee and a snack. But no, I was just wondering how last night was. I'm actually in a bit of a rush, have plans with someone." He winks "But I figured I'd stop in and see you quick." He gets up and puts his coat on. "Well thank you for coming over with coffee and a chocolate croissant. And for taking Jack out, I am likely going to go for a run today, it's been a while and I think I need to clear my head." We say our goodbyes and I go change into my running gear.

***

I clip Jack's leash onto his collar "you ready for a run boy?" He wags his tail and lets out a quick woof. We exit the building and head out. We get to the park, and I start to jog as I put an earphone in, I like to leave one out so that I can still pay attention to what's happening around me.

Last night was really something, I cannot get Olivia out of my head, everything about her just seemed perfect. Her ass, tits, body in general was just amazing and her personality was spot on. I need someone that will spar with me, and I think I have finally met her.

Erik may be the older twin by a whole two minutes, but I was always the one that oversaw things. He liked to goof off and have fun, which it fine, everyone needs to have fun. But throughout high school I started to notice a change in him, I think that was the same time he really started to take a liking towards girls. He was the typical heartbreaker in school, I could have been too if I wanted to, but that was never the life for me. I was always the one with the girlfriend, he was the one getting laid by a different girl every week I was the one making out with the same girlfriend on the couch of our parents' house.

He lost his virginity before I did, not a shocker there, he seemed to do everything before I did. He is a very responsible human, don't get him wrong, he just isn't the settling down type, I'm sure one day he'll find that girl that knocks him on his ass, I can't wait to see that day come around and meet that girl.

We get back to the beginning of the park and I slow us to a walk to bring our breathing down as we head home.

When we arrive, I give Jack a cup of food and some treats for being such a good boy and jump in the shower.

My mind drifts towards Olivia and I do not have a choice but to rub one out so that my hard-on will go away.

Chapter Seven:
Olivia

Ugh, this date cannot come soon enough, it's not that I'm not excited. I just do not want to go out with yet another guy that thinks throwing his money around is going to impress me. I do not care if you work at a clothing store in the mall, as long as you're a nice guy. I have met too many rich guys to last me a lifetime and wasn't looking forward to dating another one.

Six years ago

"Your chariot awaits my dear" Tristan holds out his hand for me. I took it graciously still in shock that Tristan Callaghan asked me out on a date! Me! He walked me to the limo waiting outside my house while my dad watched through the window. I begged him not to embarrass me and he begrudgingly agreed.
I was a ball of nerves as we walked and I was not really listening to what Tristan was talking about, it was all surreal. He snapped his fingers at the driver "I'm not paying you to just stand there Jeffery, open the damn door" Tristan snapped again as Jeffery rushed to open the car door for me.

"I could have gotten the door for myself..." I whispered quietly and gave Jeffery an apologetic smile.

He smiled and nodded to me and after Tristan joined me in the limo, Jeffery shut the door.

"I apologize darling, good help can be so hard to find, I will be sure father hears of this" Tristan shook his head glaring at Jeffery before raising the partition.

"It's really fine Tristan, he didn't need to open the door for me I have working hands."

"Nonsense! No beautiful girl of mine should ever have to lift a finger or open her own doors, it's just not right." Tristan took my hand and brought it to his lips. I felt a little more at ease and his kiss left my skin tingling. We talked mainly about him but to me it did not matter what we talked about, he was with me, and nothing could ruin that at all.

We went to the most expensive restaurant in town, I felt underdressed and out of place, don't teenagers typically go out for burgers and a movie on a first date? At the table he snapped his fingers at the waiter and nodded towards my chair, again just like Jeffery the waiter rushed to pull my chair out for me to sit.

This was a little too much for my taste, dad raised me to treat others the way I wanted to be treated. I politely smiled and said thank you as I sat down, Tristan laughed.

"Oh, my dear do not waste your breath on the help, I will handle this."

Tristan ordered me a salad and eggplant parmesan for my meal.

"Um... I'm allergic to eggplant actually" I was fiddling with my napkin that was sitting on my lap.

"OH! I am sorry" He snaps his fingers again as the waiter comes over.

"What would you like darling, the sky is the limit."

I picked up my menu and looked "I will take the herb crusted halibut, please" I smiled and handed the waiter my menu.

"No, no, no this won't do, I don't want to kiss a fish at the end of the night" He pauses to look at the menu "She will have the chicken instead. I would also like the most expensive bottle of wine you have, I do not care what it is. If it's expensive it must be good."

The waiter peered at him, then looked at me, shook his head and walked away, he clearly did not want to argue with him about our age. This date was not going as planned. More small talk was made before the waiter came over "took you long enough, you better pour it as well, for the price I'm paying to eat here." Tristen seemed to really like to throw his weight around, I am not sure how I feel about this. Why did my father have to set this up for me? He is not my type at all, but my dad wanted me to try, so here we are.

The salad he ordered for me turned out to be pretty good, however it was nothing special and likely not worth what he was paying for it, not that he cared. The chicken entrée however I was not a fan of and instead I found myself moving it around my plate more than eating it.

"What? What is wrong with your meal? Didn't your parents ever teach you to eat what is put in front of you? Come on now, I brought you here and I expect you to eat the food!"

I looked up at him shocked that he had said that to me, I did not order this for myself, he did. I wanted the fish, and he would not let me so instead I ended up with this dish that I didn't enjoy. He could suffer with the cost of it, it is not like he couldn't afford it. "I don't really like chicken; I find it bland. That's why I wanted the fish." I say quietly, afraid that he will lash out at me.

Just then the waiter comes back and asks if we would like dessert, I am just about to order a piece of chocolate cake when Tristen pipes up "does it look like she needs dessert? No, I do not think so. Just the bill will be fine and be quick about it we have other things to do." My eyes fall to the table as I drop my hands into my lap, I love dessert it is the best part of the meal.

When I think back to our first date together, I wonder how I ever agreed to a second one. Was I insane? I mean clearly, I had lost my senses, who in their right mind would want to be with someone like that?

But somehow, he ended up in my life and it was, well not good, decent, I guess you could say... He always knew what to say to me when I was feeling uncomfortable, he treated everyone around him like garbage and distracted me with sweet words and kisses. I was clearly delusional, but sometimes that is what happens when you think you're in love, you're in an abusive relationship, which I was at the time. Nowadays, I think back to this time, and I am so happy that he left me, at the time I was distraught, but it is the best thing that could have happened to me. It showed me how to think for myself and not get too close to men. That is why I have best friends.

It also helped me realize that I was not getting anything but sex from him, which honestly was not that good. I would get off once every fourth or fifth time and that was a fluke where he just happened to find the right spot occasionally. I tried playing with myself during, to see if that helped, I also tried toys and that did not work either. I ended up coming to the conclusion that it was him. Then when I started doing one-night stands and I was able to get off even if they did not really seem to know what they were doing, it took some practice though. Now however, I can get off every time, even if I am getting myself off with BOB's assistance.

Chapter Eight:
Damon

Nothing was distracting me today; all I could think about was how much I wanted this date to hurry up and get here. When I first saw her, I automatically wanted to throw her over my shoulder and take her back to my place, but something tells me Olivia is more deserving than that, not only is she beautiful, but she is also quick witted and smart. I want to cherish her for everything she was worth. I had decided that I was taking her to the aquarium to have a private tour and dinner, it's one of my favourite places. It costs a lot to rent out the whole place but it's worth it in order for a person to enjoy some me time. There weren't many women I could ask for help with creating a menu, so I asked Stacy, my assistant. She had told me that I likely couldn't go wrong with either a nice fish dinner, or a steak and that as long as I followed it up with a chocolate dessert, I should be golden. So that's exactly what I did, I called up the aquarium and got to work on placing the order for us when we arrived. Next was to figure out which day we would go out, and where I could pick her up from.

Damon
Hey beautiful, its Damon. I'm wondering what date works for you this week so that I can finish putting plans together.

I waited for hours for a reply, it seemed, she must be really busy making sure everything was wrapped up after the event they hosted. Just after lunch I received a message.

Olivia
Friday will work best.

That's it? That's all I get? I waited 3 hours for 4 words!? I figured I would have gotten a little more than that.

Damon
Okay, I'll pick you up at 5pm, if you'll just give me your address, please.

Olivia
I'll meet you there, where are we going?

Damon
Are you sure? It's no problem to pick you up or get my driver to. We're going to the aquarium.

Olivia

Really? The aquarium? That seems a little childish but ok. I know where that is, I'll meet you there. See you then.

Well, I guess I was just dismissed on text message, that sucks. If she didn't want to go out on a date, why did she agree to put herself in the auction?

I finish up what I'm doing and call up the aquarium on my way home to set up my reservation, they are thrilled that I'm coming back again. I typically do this once a year at least, sometimes it's just me though. Everyone seems to want to be my friend because I have money, except Olivia, she seems to hate me because I have money, or because I won a date with her, I'm not sure.

I've become good friends with the staff over the years, it's become one of favourite places. I'm always sure to tip well, I always give them enough to cover dinner for the staff working that night as well as donate $5000 to put towards a charity of their choice to help various fish.

To have her date the idea of going there so much without even going yet sets me off a bit, I hope she will be able to see why it's one of my favourite places to be, maybe it can become our spot.

Chapter Nine:
Olivia

I zipped up my black dress and adjusted my thigh highs, I stepped in front of my full-length mirror happy with the results. This date may have come as a result for the charity auction, but I'll be dammed if I don't get lucky tonight, a girl has needs after all. I adjusted my curls, so they draw attention to my chest, I had my fuck me bra on underneath that no one could look away from. My phone vibrates on the top of my dresser, it was Damon, my heart fluttered a little bit seeing it, he had given me the address for our date just in case. I quickly applied red lipstick and walked out to the living room to get my heels.

I was greeted with a collective 'damn!' from my friends as I did a 360 twirl for them. "If he doesn't fuck you tonight I will" Aly said blowing me a kiss.

I laughed "I may take you up on that" I winked back at her.

"Where is he taking you tonight?! I bet it is somewhere so romantic" Chellsea sighed. She has her date next weekend with Michael and hasn't stopped talking about him since. I truly do hope for her it turns out well. "It looks like we are going to the aquarium?" I was a little shocked, I hardly knew Damon, but I expected something fancier. Oh well, this date is for the kids, and I know there will not be a second let alone happily ever after like Chellsea wants. I got a notification that my car had arrived, I slipped on my heels, and I blew my friends a kiss.

I was still surprised he chose the aquarium of all places; I used to come here all the time with my dad when I was little but never thought of it as a date location. I expected something like the blue water café for sushi but not the aquarium.

Damon met me at my uber, he smiled at me and took my hand and led me to the entrance. The entire place was empty "I rented out the entire building we will be having dinner on the top floor" Ah there it was, the rich man flex I knew they were all the same. We made our way to the top floor where there was a single table laid out. We were surrounded by jellyfish and the tanks gave a blue glow throughout the room, there was the money I was expecting. It was pretty as well though, it was starting to grow on me, I understood why he picked this place to have dinner.

He pulled out my chair for me and then went around to his side where a waiter was waiting with a nice bottle of white wine chilled. The waiter showed us the bottle and we graciously accepted, well he opened it and gave us a taste. I think this was the best wine I've ever tasted, and it made me wonder how much he spent on this one bottle of wine. I could taste the hints of undertones of the citrus, and I may have let out a little moan, which both the waiter and Damon took as a sign that I enjoyed it, which resolved in them filling my glass.

"Do you mind if I order for us, or would you prefer to order for yourself?" Damon asked me sweetly as we clinked glasses in cheers.

"You can order for us, I don't think I would be able to decide" At least he asked my permission unlike Tristan, I thought to myself.

"Perfect, I placed the order before we got here and I'm hoping you are going to love it!"

Then I see a waiter come out with some side plates in one hand and a covered dish in another. He sets a plate in front of each of us and then takes the cover off to reveal a delicious smelling plate of shrimp scampi frittata. "Thank you, Simon." He says to the waiter. This was new, a polite rich guy.

I felt like giving him a hard time. "Are you really serving me fish in front of fish?"

"Yes, I know it's a little weird, but I love this dish. It's one of my favorites and when it's done right you can't say no." Damon answers me with a sexy smirk. Damn him and that smile.

I take my first shrimp onto my fork, dip it in the garlic butter and place it on my tongue. I think I may have a little bit of an orgasm, oh my god he wasn't kidding about it being amazing. Damn rich people and their money always getting the best things!

"Oh my god, this is so good" I say to Damon and a reach for more shrimp to shove into my face.

"I'm glad you approve my dear!"

We make some small talk before our Caesar salads come out, wow he really is flaunting this money on this date. But I mean, as long as I get to eat a great meal and have sex, I'm good.

"So, what do you do for fun Olivia?"

"I hang out with my girls a lot, we do morning coffee every second morning, if not every day. And we hangout sometimes in the evenings. I also have a pet fish named Bubbles that I have conversations with."

"You defiantly have a different personality then I pegged you for, but I like it!" Damon says before taking another sip of wine.

For supper we are brought out a beautiful steak cooked to a perfect medium rare with Parmesan broccoli and garlic mashed potatoes, on top there is also a stick of the shrimp scampi from before. My mouth waters just with the smells alone, I can honestly say that even when I was with Tristen, he never took me to places where they cooked good food. I am very impressed!

"If you keep moaning while eating, I don't think I'll be able to continue to act like a gentleman."

"I never said you had to; I'm planning on having sex tonight. It just depends on whether it's with you or someone else." I give him a quirky smile and wink before I take a sip of my wine.

Damon chokes on his last sip of wine and Simon comes running over to make sure he's OK. He waves them off, silently reassuring them that he's fine. "Oh wow, okay! I thought we would wait for the next date at least; I would love to take you home tonight. You are quite forward about what you want, it's refreshing to see in a woman."

Just then two chocolate lava cakes come out on a plate looking amazing. This man has me all figured out and he doesn't even know me yet, I can only imagine how it'll be when he does. Shit! Why am I thinking about things like this? I'm only out with his man because he won this date at an auction and I want to bang his brains out, that's it! Nothing else, maybe at some point we could become fuck buddies but other than that nothing is going to happen between us!

Once dessert is done, we decide to take a walk through the aquarium.

I was enjoying the night so far, the food was amazing, and the wine gave me a nice little buzz. The nice thing about being with a billionaire that rented out the entire place too was that we were able to take our wine with us. We walked through the aquarium surrounded by ocean life animals I felt at peace and enjoyed Damon's company. We walked in step with each other in comfortable silence for a while.

"So, we established that I got you pegged wrong from first impressions, what do you think of me?" Damon asked

I laughed "I figured you are just like every other rich guy, flaunts their money to impress the girl and hope they can buy their love."

Damon looked like I slapped him in the face "I am definitely not like that!"

I smirked "That's what they all say, then when you do fall in love with the person not the money, they feel you're not good enough and break your heart".

Went a little too close to the heart with that one but it is true, rich men are a type and you should always keep your heart protected from them.

"Well, I am not like that, I won't lie I wanted to impress you tonight, but I can tell you that my money does not define who I am as a person, and I can prove it to you" there was some urgency in his voice.

"Oh, can you?" This piqued my interest.

He nodded "Yes, go on a second date with me and I can show you I am more than my money"

I grimaced "Nah, I will take your word on it, I do not to second dates." I started walking a little further ahead from him to look at the penguins.

"I will double my donation if you go on a second date with me!" Was that panic in his voice? I was stunned at $40,000 for two dates, are you kidding me?

"That's not helping your image right now" I smirked at him.

"Come on, what do you have to lose?" he asked. I Considered the question; I really didn't have anything to lose.

"Ok, deal I will go on a second date with you so you can show me you are more than your money."

We shook hands and continued our way through the aquarium.

"Why the aquarium?" I asked, even though he rented out the whole place, it was still an odd choice.

Damon was quite for a moment "Honestly?" he asked.

"Yeah honestly" I replied.

"Well, when I was younger my parents didn't have a lot of money but once a year, they would bring my brother and I here for the day, this place has a close place to my heart. Since then, it has stuck with me, I come here by myself all the time and I wanted to be able to share it with someone else, I thought you were worth it. As I'm sure you have noticed I know the staff's names. I made sure that they were tipped well tonight, had supper for themselves and I donated $5000 to the charity they're sponsoring now."

My heart melted a little bit and I felt like a dick for the comment I made about him not being more than his money. I nodded thoughtfully "that is really sweet." He smiled at me and took my hand as we walked outside to look at the otters.

The stars were high in the sky and the night was mild, I shivered walking to the exhibit, Damon took his coat off and wrapped it around me.

"So, tell me a little bit about yourself, do you have any siblings? Pets? Hobbies?"

I look at him "I have one brother, Xander, he was actually at the auction, he's the one that bid $8000 on me to bump up the prize money and see if you were serious. But I have 3 best friends that are like sisters to me. We ended up renovating our house so that we all live together without having to walk outside. My dad passed away shortly after my high school graduation and after that my mom moved across the country, we didn't talk much anymore. As you know I have a pet fish named Bubbles. And I like to bake and cook."

"You must feel really passionate about your friends and family, you light up when you talk about them, tell me more. Should I be concerned that your brother bid on you at the auction?" Damon answers with a slight laugh. We walked along the pavilion to the dolphin exhibition.

"You should be concerned for yourself, he is very protective of me, especially after we lost our father. I wouldn't be surprised if he's practicing his 'don't hurt my girl' speech already. As for my friends let's see, their names are Marina, Chellsea and Alexis but we call her Aly. Marina is the one who I live with directly, we've known each other since, well forever really. She is a bartender at the pub down the street from our house, she even met her boyfriend there. If I had to warn you of one of them it would be her, she's not afraid to tell you get fucked and how to get there. Chellsea is a hopeless romantic and seems to think that I am going to end up falling in love with you on this date. She works with me and comes from a really broken past. She was auctioned off as well, and I believe her date is next week. I'm really hoping it goes well otherwise I will have to load up on the ice cream. Aly is the DYI handy girl of our group; she has red hair and is a firecracker. Has tons of tattoos and owns a renovation company, she actually helped with the renovations of our house."

Damon looks down at me and smiles "They sound lovely, and I can't wait to meet them. I feel a little prone to say that I'm liking Chellsea the most right now since she's already gunning for us to make it" he gives me a sexy wink as we move onto another part of the aquarium.

I laugh "Ha, I should have figured when I said that that you would say something like that. What about you?"

"Well let's see, I have a brother, he's the same age as me. He is a playboy by heart, always looking for a new girl to bed. I also have a husky named Jack, he is adorable, and I can't wait for you to meet him, assuming you like dogs, that is. As for hobbies I enjoy playing the guitar."

"Wow, okay I didn't peg you to have animals or a hobby outside of work."

We finish at the aquarium, and I am led to a limo where a driver waits with the door open. I turn to look at Damon "All the stops I see?"

He lets out a small laugh "I did tell you I was trying to show you a good time tonight, this just adds to the experience."

We get to the limo, and he helps me inside "Would you like to go home are do you want to hang out a little longer?" He gives me a sweet smile.

I look him straight in the eye "We could go back to your house and have sex?"

"Not tonight, as much as I would like to, I don't want you to get the impression that that's the only reason I bid for you, because it in no way is. I want to get to know you and I want you to fall for me, if you can. So how about a take you home for the night and we will talk during the week about our next date?"

I sign "Okay. I guess I might have to take Aly up on her offer after all."

"What do you mean?" He asks.

"Well, she told me that if you didn't fuck me tonight, she would. So like I said, one way or another I'm getting laid." I wink at him.

"Interesting friends you have…" he says confused.

"It's just something girls say to each other." Five minutes later we arrived at what I told the was my house, little does he know we are a street over. He gets out of the car and reaches for my hand, which I accept and get out. Damon wraps his arms around me and tilts my chin up towards him, my breath catches as our lips touch.

I melted into his arms and temporarily thought about inviting him in, when I realized we were not actually at my house. When the kiss ended, he smiles down at me. "Can I walk you to your down?" His voice was husky, and I could tell he wanted more.

I pushed him away and shook my head. "Not tonight, I also forgot my key, so I need to go in through the back." He looked disappointed but smiled anyways and kissed me one more time. I wanted to melt into him and stay on his lips forever. His lips were like a drug sending me into a buzz.

"Good night beautiful, text me." He climbed back into the limo, I gave a small wave and turned to walk down the bike bath to my 'back yard.' I waited for his car to leave and walked to my house.

I kicked off my heels and walked to my room and got into some comfy clothes.

Damon

Can't wait for our next date. Sweet dreams beautiful.

I was still feeling his kiss on my lips. This man is going to get me into trouble.

I make my way into the kitchen just as another message comes in, thinking its him again I take a peek, only to be disappointed.

Tristan

Hey Livvy, want to hook up? I miss your body and the way it did things to me. I'm sure you miss mine too.

Ugh, Tristan. I grimaced as I turn around and notice Marina.

"Woah, bad date?" She was sitting at out kitchen table, a tea sitting in front of her. No doubt she had been waiting for me to get home and dish. How I missed her when I came in, I have no idea, I must be on cloud nine, or I was. I slid my phone across the table so she could see the message on the screen. She picked it up and frowned.

"Seriously? This guy again? Does he now know when to quit?" I sit down at the table with her.

"I really don't know but I wish he would just stop." Mar grabs my phone and types out a reply.

Olivia
Sorry Tristan. I found someone else to fill my needs…
Far better then I ever got with you. -Liv.

She slides the phone back over to me so that I can see what she sent, just as another text comes in.

Tristan
What!? Who!? Was it that douchebag from the auction? YOU. ARE. MINE. You hear me? MINE! Where are you? I'm coming over now!!

I throw my hands up in the air "I give up! This is why I don't do fucking relationships!"

Marina frowned at me "I don't think that's fair Liv, not all guys are like Tristan. Don't you think maybe you should give this new guy a chance?"

Six years ago

I sat in my dad's truck looking out the passenger window watching the scenery go by. When I asked for a weekend at the cabin, he jumped into planning right away and had a plan ready to go before the end of the day. As we drove, he talked about what the plans were over the weekend.
"We are going for a hike, we can go see the waterfall, maybe do dome fishin'. What do you say Liv?"
I nodded "Yeah dad, sounds great!"
He looked over at me and cocked his eyebrow "What's going on in your mind baby girl?"
Dad always had a way to know when something was wrong, I turned to face him. "It's Tristan."
I thought back on what had happened during our first date, he was such an ass, rude and entitled. I grimaced. "I just don't think we're a good fit."
His face softens as he looks back at the road "You have only had one date with him hun, I really think you should give him another chance. Maybe he was just nervous. I won't be around forever, and I just want to see you happy."
I smiled at him "Dad, you're not going anywhere anytime soon."
He smiled back at me "Of course not, but still give the sucker a chance for me."
I reluctantly agreed and sent Tristan a text for when a second date would work.

I drummed my fingers on the table "That was the last advice my dad ever gave me you know."
Marina grabbed my hand and held it. "Your dad didn't know what kind of person Tristan was either, if he was around, he would have personally nurtured him with a rusty spoon. I know because I would have helped him."
I laughed "Yeah, you're right he would have."
Marina rubbed my hand and smiled "So come on, I have been pacing the floors all night to hear about your date, how did it go?"
We sat at the table for most of the night talking about everything else but the date, she was just going to have to wait. By the time I was ready to slip into bed I had forgotten about Tristan and his stupid messaged. I closed my eyes and went to sleep.

***

I woke up the next morning with a text that had me smiling down at my phone.

Damon
Good morning beautiful, I can't wait to see you again. I hope you feel the same way, last night was more then I could have asked for. I only wish that you would have been there when I woke up.

Olivia

I wish last night could have ended the way I was hoping as well and then who knows, maybe I would have been there when you woke up. But I guess now you'll never know.

Damon

You're sure salty this morning, aren't you?

Are you working today, or can I take you for coffee?

Olivia

No, no, no! Mr., we agreed on two dates, you're not then allowed to have 3. Unless of course you are waiting our second date to be coffee?

Hmm… doesn't seem worth it to me.

I lay in bed, staring at my beta fish on my side table, life is so much easier when you're a fish. Swimming all day, getting fed, no job and most importantly, no feelings.
"You don't have feelings do you Bubs?" Of course, he wouldn't reply but it was not fair question. He must have some feelings, I feed him everyday and he always looks at me when I come into the room. Or I think he does, anyway. More importantly why am I talking to a fish? Right, because thinking about the amazing night I had with Damon, how he kissed me last night and left me hanging just made me want him more. I knew better then to get attached that way

you will never get your heart broken. I covered my head with the covers, this was all too much. I haven't had feelings for anyone since Tristan, and no dick regardless of how amazing it is should deter me from changing my mind. I needed to get Damon out of my system. Unfortunately, the only way to do that was to fuck him, and he wanted a second date in order for that to happen.

I close my eyes and think of how blue his eyes are, how sexy his smirk is when he's being cocky and sarcastic. Mmmm, what a turn on he is to look at, such a nice piece of man. I reach up under my shirt and start playing with my breast, rubbing it, squeezing it and tweaking the nipple, wishing he was the one doing this to me now. I bring my other hand down to my panties and move them aside. I twirl my finger around my clit, starting off slow, just like I imagine Damon would. Oh, the things I imagine him doing to me, the way his fingers would feel, his tongue lapping at my nipples like it was the last meal he would ever get. I slide a finger into my heat and let out a quiet moan, it's not big enough to feel like him, so I slide another one in, but it's still not good enough. I turn over quickly and grab BOB, my trusty purple portable cock, yes, I gave my favourite vibrator a name. I shimmy out of my underwear and spread my legs. I rub BOB up the slit of my wet pussy and then slide him in. That feels much closer to how big I imagine Damon is, but it's still not the same, because it's not him.

"DAMN IT" I scream as I turn up the vibe hoping it'll help me get off. I slide it in and out of myself slowly as it vibrates, moving faster and increasing the speed. I started to gasp and moan louder. Adding my other hand into the mix I rub my clit. In my fantasy Damon knows exactly how to use his cock, just enough to tease me and make me want more. Why can't I get him out of my system? Closing my eyes, I imagine that I am riding his cock and that he is playing with my tits, starting out slowly and then increasing speed.

"Yes, yes, yes, oh right there, yes, YES!" I scream my orgasm. Panting and coming down from my high it pops into my head that Marina could have been home and heard all of that. Oh well, I think, a girl got needs, she knows!

***

I walked into the kitchen to see all my girls sitting at the table with a coffee in front of them and a mug waiting for me. They all have these creepy smiles on their faces. I grab my mug and take a swig, "mmm, oh yeah, that's good!"

Aly waits for me to put my mug down "Well…. Are you going to tell us how it was or make us suffer? I'm assuming since you didn't end up in my room last night that you got laid. Was it good?" All the girl's eyes went wide, waiting for my answer.

"No, there wasn't any sex unfortunately, you know I tried for it, but he was too worried about being a gentleman. "I roll my eyes as I take another much-needed sip of coffee.

"Oh, what a nice man you got to go on a date with! I hope mine is the same way, except I won't be trying to sleep with him on the first night." Marina looks at Chellsea and then back at me "I'm sure your date will be everything you're wanting and more. However, now we are talking about Liv's date with the sexy billionaire. Tell us more, what was he like? What did you talk about? Tell us everything."

"Well, as you all know he took me to the aquarium, he rented out the whole thing and had a private chef make us supper. I can't talk about that though, because the food was so good and if I start thinking about it again, I'll have to go and take care of myself," we all let out a giggle "after we ate, we walked around the aquarium and got to know each other better. Then he wrapped his coat around me before we got back in the limo, and he dropped me off."

"YOU LET HIM DRIVE YOU HOME?!" All three of the girls yelled at me.

"NO! I got him to drop me off a street away, he doesn't know that though..." I say as I stare into my cup, afraid to look up and see the disappointment in my girls' faces.

Marina is the first one to pipe up "We know that you have an issue with relationships, especially with rich guys, but it's not fair to lump them all into one group."

"Yeah, come on! He was obviously trying hard to impress you and not make you feel like you did with Tristen." Chellsea just had to get her two cents in.

"I hope you are at least seeing him again...?" Aly asks.

"Yes, I told him I would go on another date with him. He told me he would double his donation if I did. So of course, I couldn't deny the children." All my girls stare at me with huge eyes and their mouths wide open "Oh my god! This guy must really like you! That's what $40,000 for two dates?"

"I know, I know. This time he said he would show me his laid-back side. So, we'll see what he considers that to be."

"When is it?" Asks Aly.

"I don't know. I'm trying to get out of it, you know I don't do second dates." I say looking into my cup of coffee again, I just know that if I look up, I will see 3 disappointed faces staring back at me, I hate disappointing my girls.

Marina starts "I think you should give him a chance; you don't seem to have the same feelings you did when you went on a date with Tristan do you?"

"Well, no" I stamper.

Chellsea pops in with her two cents "Well then there you go, give him a chance to show you he's different. Did he give you any reason to doubt him?"

"No, he was very sweet. He told me he even made sure all the staff working last night were fed on his dim."

"Awwwwww" all the girls say together. Then Aly finishes with "well then there you go, that's settled. You're going and were not going to allow you to tell him no. Even if we have to hog tie you and deliver you to him wrapped in a bow."

I frown at them, sadly I know they aren't lying. They would do that, so I guess that means I'm going on that second date. Doesn't mean I can't make him work for it first.

Chapter Ten:
Damon

I lay in bed, my eyes open, Jack beside me still sleeping. Some days I wish I could be a dog; they really have it made. They get to sleep all day, they're awake what? Maybe a couple hours every day? Other then that they sleep a lot, go to the bathroom, eat, drink, maybe play some ball. That's it, on the other side though they must be lonely, that's why their so happy to see us when we come home from work or wherever else we are.

I must get up and head into the office today, but I'd rather spend my day with Jack or Olivia. Erik will be at the office, or he should be, so I'll see him no matter what.
I jump in the shower and for what feels like the millionth time my mind drifts to Olivia, here we go again, time to get rid of this problem again. I wonder if ill ever tire of her, I don't think so. I can't imagine doing so, when I can finally call her mine, I will cherish that woman, that's what she deserves. I silently curse myself for not bringing her home. I would love to take her on every surface of my apartment. I know that's all she wants, but I need to find a way to show her how I can be different than the others.

When I get to the office, I pull out my phone and ask if she wants to have lunch, I need to see her again. Last night wasn't enough, I don't think I'll ever have enough. She said she can't see me today though, so I guess it's just me and Erik. The office is dead on the weekends, I let everyone have the day off, but I come in to catch up on some things. It's quiet then, I reply to some emails and look at charity's that may have popped up over the weekend that I could help.

"Hey, I wasn't expecting to see you here today, thought you'd be with your girlfriend" Erik says as he pops his head into my office.
"Come on, I'm here every weekend, it's the time I use to catch up on things."
Erik walks into my office and sits down across from my desk. "You know, it wouldn't hurt you to take a few days off, enjoy your life..."
"I do enjoy my life, just because I'm working doesn't mean I don't like what I do. I helped get us this place did I not?"
"You did, I'm not saying you didn't. I'm just saying I can't remember the last time you took even one day to yourself; you know, sit at home and just watch a movie or something. Your always on the run somewhere."
"You don't know what I do every minute of the day you know; I do exist when you're not around."
"If you say so. Hey, you want to get some burritos for lunch today? On me."

"Sounds good." He walks out of my office, and I place the order for our lunch to be delivered at 12:15pm.

Damon
I can't stop thinking about you… do you want to talk about our second date now? What day works for you?

Olivia
I was thinking after I got home last night. I really don't do the whole second date thing. Can we just call it quits with that?

No way was I loosing already, she didn't even let me show her all my personality.

Damon
Did I do something? I'd really like to continue our plan to have the second date… plus I already paid the other $20,000 I said I would.

Olivia
Ugh, of course you did. You move fast, don't you? Although not to fast considering you wouldn't go for sex last night…

Damon
Believe me, its not that I didn't want it, I was just trying to show you respect. I'm not in this just for sex, I want to get to know you and possibly have a relationship with you.

Olivia
I'm not a relationship girl, I told you that. So, I say we have sex, see if were a good fit ▯ and then possibly turn into fuck buddies, that's the closest to a 'relationship' you're getting out of me.

Damon
You know, most girls would love to be in a relationship with me.

Olivia
I'm sure anyone of them would love to be in a relationship with your wallet too. But you don't see me signing up for that!

Damon
Please just give me the second date and if you still want nothing to do with me then ill stop trying.

Olivia
Fine... I'm pretty busy though, so we'll have to talk dates later. Now go away, I have work to do.

I groaned and put my phone down, I need to make this second date perfect. I thought back to what my brother had said. Although I enjoy what I do for work, he's right I don't take days off. I will need to put some serious thought into this.

Chapter Eleven:
Olivia

I don't want to admit this to myself or the girls, but I really do see myself being able to fall for Damon. I don't want it though, so I'm going to keep this to myself for now. Shouldn't be a problem tonight, all the girls are out doing things, so I have the house to myself. Just me and BOB! I need to keep myself in check, feelings lead to broken hearts, and I be dammed if I find myself sitting on my front step crying again.

***

I sit down at my desk the next morning and I hear my phone go off. I quickly check it; I try not to answer it to much when I'm at work because I'm on the clock. Once in a while I need a quick two-minute break though, plus I haven't really started working yet. I don't typically work on weekends, but after a function there's a lot to wrap up, so the company asks us to work an extra day and gives us a gift card to get lunch. Its really important to like the company you work for, and I definitely do.

Damon
Good morning beautiful, have you decided when I can see you again?

I try so hard not to respond to him because he keeps pushing. I don't know how many times I can tell him that I don't do the dating thing and I also don't do second dates. The only reason I've agreed to it is because he agreed to double his contribution to the charity.

Olivia
Why are you so adamant to see me?

Don't you have any friends?

Damon
I do. I also have a brother and a dog. But that doesn't mean I can't see more than one of them a week. Otherwise, I would only ever see my dog, I mean he would be happy about that. I don't think my brother or friends would be though. Or my mom for that matter.

Oh, he's got jokes this morning! I like this side of him, do you think it's possible that he has found a way under my skin? What if he has broken me of my stride? Wait! What am I thinking? This isn't some stupid fairy-tale princess romance novel, this is real life. Shit like that doesn't happen to real people, you find someone and hope that they're a good person, otherwise you get fucked over and turn into me. Sad but true.

Olivia
That doesn't answer my question….

Damon

Okay, fine. I want to get to know you more. I don't know how many times I must tell you this. Plus, I paid $20,000 for another date, so I need to make sure I get the date part out of it.

Olivia

Or we could forget the money and the second date, and you can be on your way with your merry dog and brother.

Damon

Come on, you told me I could show you my laid-back side. I would really like to do that!

Olivia

Let's put it on the back burner for now, I'm not ready to commit to a second date.

Damon

Or we could go out tonight? Nothing says laid back like making plans for the night of, right?

Olivia

Can't tonight, girl's night!

Damon

Oh? Is it just like on TV and in movies? Pillow fights in your underwear and lots of romance movies?

Really though, that's exciting. What are you girls doing tonight? I could bring over some wine and snacks for you if you'd like?

Olivia
Yes, just like you see on TV and in movies, except there's no underwear, were completely naked. Sorry, to disappoint you on that front! We're getting Chellsea ready for her date tonight, she's really excited about it and it's a ritual.

Damon
Oh, that sounds fun! I won't invade on your girl's night ritual. I will however keep "bugging" you until I get that second date though!

It was just announced at the office that we are to start planning the charity event for the pet shelter that will be happening in three months from now. This is another one that hits close to home, I love how the company always makes your heart melt with who they choose to represent. My job is to start figuring out what we are going to do, where we should have it. Since it's a pet charity maybe we should have a pet adoption event where people can come and adopt the abandoned animals. I think that would go over well, plus it helps the charity out in more ways than one.

"Are you ready to go?" Chellsea appears out of nowhere and scares me, we spend time together on our lunch break since we work together. But usually, I'm the one picking her up, I must have really gotten into my work.

"Yeah, sure let me grab my purse." I say as I stand up and reach for my coat and purse from the coat rack.

"Can someone please tell me where I can find a ….. Miss….. Olivia Hendrix."

I turn around to see a short stubby man holding the most beautifully wrapped basket I've ever seen.

"Oh, um. Hi, that's me." I say to him with a quick wave.

"This is for you" he says as he hands me the basket. "Its from a …. Mr. Thomson."

I turn and look at Chellsea, she has stars in her eyes, she's such a romantic. "Of course, it is, thank you! Here let me give you a tip" I say as I reach into my purse to grab my wallet after handing the basket to Chellsea.

"Oh, that's not necessary, it's been taken care of already. Thank you though, I hope you have a great day. You have a good man there miss."

I put my wallet back in my purse and turn to see Chellsea sitting at my deck in front of the basket trying to figure out what's in it without opening it.

"Yes, we can open it." I say as I step closer and untie the ribbon at the top, it's almost to beautiful to unwrap.

Inside there are 3 bottles of wine, one red, one white, and one rose, guess he wanted to cover all the bases. There is also a fancy box of truffles, along with various other snacks, a gift card for a takeout meal on him, 4 different types of underwear, and a note.

I didn't know which types you and your girls like to wear so I got a selection. ▯
-Damon

"Umm, why is there underwear in there."
Chellsea looks at me confused. "Does he think we all go commando?"
I laugh "No! I was talking to him this morning about how we have naked pillow fights because he asked if we had them in our underwear, I told him I was sorry to ruin that fantasy. So, this is his way of telling me I can justify it. What a smart ass! Let's go for lunch, I'm hungry, we'll bring this down to the car on the way out."
"He's so sweet, why can't you just give in to him and go out with him again? He's really trying here."
"You know why. I don't do second dates. I don't want to go there again." I looked down at the basket and smiled despite myself, I will admit this was very sweet.
"Yeah, but I don't know Liv, every time it's brought up you just say, 'it's the way it is' and that's that" Chellsea put her hands on her hips.
"I..." Damn she was right.

I sighed "Fine, you got me. Come on let's go for lunch and I will fill you in."

***

After lunch, Chellsea went back to her desk in a daze. Honestly, I don't believe there's a chance in hell of me being in a relationship, I hope this hasn't tainted her take on relationships. The rest of the day finishes slowly, I can't wait to get home and start girl's night.

***

We arrive home after work with the gift basket and head to the kitchen table to set it down. "Oh, what's this? Do you have a secret admirer?" Aly says.

"Actually, we all do, because this is for all of us. I told Damon that we were having a girl's night in order to get Chellsea ready for her date and he sent this to the office."

"It was so sweet of him, look at all this stuff!! I hope my date is just like him, you got really lucky with this one Liv." Chellsea says to me. "I'm going to start with a shower, then ill come out and we can start on the magic." She says as she sashays down the hall towards the shower.

 "Okay, lets see what's in this baby" Marina says as she squeals with excitement. "Oh my god, Olivia, this wine alone is worth a small fortune. And he got one of each type!"

"I'll grab the wine glasses, I picked us up a meat plater as well and some vegetables for a snack. Yum!!" Aly pipes in.

"Okay, so which bottle do we want to open first?" Chellsea says as she heads towards us in her towel, freshly showered.

"Let's start with the red I think that way if it spills you won't be all ready yet and well have to start over again." I chime in. "I want to take a picture and send it to him to thank him for the gift."

"Sounds good to me." Marina says as she opens the cork from the bottle and starts pouring the glasses, but we have to have a glass of wine in hand first.

Olivia
Sent an image.

Thank you for the gift basket, the girls had a good laugh about the underwear. So, thanks for making me tell them that story!

Also, you got my name wrong by the way.

Damon
You're welcome. I wanted to make sure you thought about me even if I couldn't be there. Go enjoy your girl's night and ill talk to you later.

Oh, I'm sorry. What is it?

Olivia
It's Harper, but your forgiven. You have excellent taste in wine, I might add.

I turned on some music and told Chellsea to bring out the outfits she was thinking about wearing before we started on makeup. I sipped on my wine; I didn't want to get too drunk before helping Chellsea do her makeup. She knew how to do it herself, but this has become our tradition, one of us gets a date and we all help whoever it is get ready and properly send them off. Then the ones left behind order in food, drink some more and enjoy the night.

Chellsea looked gorgeous in a tight fitted red dress, I gave her a smokey eye dramatic look and Marina curled her dark brown hair. She looked beautiful. There was a knock on the door when she was ready, perfect timing!

I opened the door to see Chellsea's date, he didn't look as nice as he did at the charity event. He wore dark jeans and a button-down shirt with the top two buttons undone so you could see his chest hair poke out. I frowned but hoped that looks were deceiving. Personally, I didn't like chest hair on a man, especially to that extent. But this wasn't my date, so my opinion doesn't matter.

"I'm here to pick up...uhm..." He stammered

"Chellsea." I finished his sentence

"Yes! That's her name, Chellsea." He smiled looking at me up and down. I snapped a glare at him, and he straightened up.

"I'm coming! Let me grab my coat" Chellsea sang and floated by ready to leave. He looked at her and grinned. Chellsea waved goodbye and took off with her knight in shining tin foil and I closed the door.

"He better treat her well tonight" I walked to the table to pour myself another glass of wine.

"I'm sure he will, don't be so cynical" Aly said as she flopped on the couch with a takeout menu.

I downed my glass of wine and opened the white. I decided not to argue and just enjoy this fantastic gift basket. When I took a sip of the white, I recognized that it was the same one Damon and I shared at the aquarium, I smiled looking at the bottle.

"What got you all giddy?" Marina poked at me. I looked up and handed her the bottle.

"This is what I had the other night with Damon, its really good" My heart fluttered a little bit and felt warm and fuzzy.

"I like the side he is bringing out of you" She poured herself a glass.

"You mean you like the side the wine is bringing out of me" I laughed and finished my glass holding out for another one.

Marina rolled her eyes at me and poured another glass.

After the wine was gone, I was far passed tipsy. The girls had gone to bed, and I made my way to my room laying on my bed with the stuffed otter Damon got me. I looked over to my phone and against my best judgement I decided to text Damon.

Olivia
This otter is so damn cute.

Damon
You're up pretty late, but I'm glad you like it.

Olivia
It's your fault I'm up so late with your fancy ass gift basket.

Damon
Haha oh?

Olivia
Mhmm... So much wine and snacks and wine.

Damon
Are you drunk right now?

Olivia
Maybe I am, maybe I'm not, you will never know.

Damon
Well just make sure you drink some water and maybe take an aspirin.

Olivia
Look at you Mr. Fancy pants taking care of me, you're crazy.

Damon
Why am I crazy? I'd love to take care of you.

Olivia
Because you're wasting your time, I'm not relationship material.

                                                         Damon
Regardless of what you think, I am not wasting my time on you... I think you would be the best girlfriend ever.

Olivia
Because I put out?

                                                         Damon
No, my dear, because you are perfect.

I'm glad it was such a hit!

Olivia
How did you get it to my office so fast?

                                                         Damon
Ahh, sorry my dear I can't share my secrets ▨

Olivia
Ugh fine I will just contact the delivery guy, he did give me his number.

I snickered to myself, let him stew in that for a while, but then I realized he would probably send off a email to the company and I didn't want to get anyone in trouble.

Olivia
Just kidding!

Damon
You're such a smart ass! Go to sleep sweetheart, I will text you tomorrow.

I put my phone down back on the charger, he is so delusional. I rolled over and pulled my blanket up over me, I snuggled the otter and drifted off to sleep with a huge smile on my face.

Chapter Twelve:
Damon

I looked at the picture Olivia sent me last night and smiled at it. She loved it enough to send me a message. She never initiates the conversation. Half the time I can't even get her to answer the ones I send her.

It's a picture of her and her friends enjoying the gift basket I got delivered to her office after she told me it was girls' night.

It was from a cute mom and pop shop down the street from my office, that's where I get all my baskets from, it helps them stay in business and they are good on the fly. I called the store and told them what I needed, and they delivered, even had it delivered to her for me in less than half an hour.

I smiled at the message she sent me, to be honest this could have gone either way. She could have chastised me for crossing a line, but no she loved it! I won't lie I didn't just send the gift basket because I felt like being nice, I wanted Olivia to see that not only will I respect her need for girl time but will encourage and spoil her at the same time.

This girl will be the death of me for sure. I put my phone on the charger and crawled into bed.

The next morning, I get up, have a shower and make my way into work, nothing to exciting is happening today. I'm looking up potential businesses to invest in. I have Stacy call and set up a time to meet with them well I continue to research them. I just found one that works regularity with pit bulls, animals are something I'm passionate about so I would be interested in pursuing this. Sometimes I buy the company, other times I just invest or become a silent partner, it all depends on the company.

"Stacy, can you come in here for a minute please." I call out, but I don't hear anything back. I figure she's just busy closing something up, so I wait a few minutes and then go in search of her. But when I walk out of my office her desk is empty.

Stacy has been very absent lately; I can never seem to find her when I need her. I look around quickly to see if maybe she's just walking back from the bathroom or getting a coffee. But that's not the case, I don't see her anywhere. I head over to another employee's desk and ask when the last time they saw her was. I don't like the answer, according to them Stacy has been gone for over an hour.

"Well, I guess I'll just do it myself then" I say to no one in particular and head back into my office.

I sit down in my chair and pull up the information again and dial.

"Hello, you've reached pity's-r-us how may I help you?" Says a chipper girl that can't possibly be older than 18.

"Hello, I'm wondering if the owner is around?"

"Sure, one second, let me put you on hold real quick."

I never enjoyed being put on hold, having to listen to that stupid elevator music, or worse, nothing at all and then you just think that you were hung up on. I've been waiting for almost two minutes now and I am just about to hang up when an older sounding man picks up.

"Hello, sir. How may I help you?"

"Hello, this is Damon Thompson, I'm sure you've heard of me before. Someone from your company emailed me asking if I would be willing to help out so I figured we could set up a time to meet and see if I would be able to help you or not."

"Oh yes, of course, sir. I would love to set up a time. Anytime works for me really, I can come to your office, or you can come here."

"How about you come here, and we can talk business? Say next Monday at 10am?"

"Sounds perfect. Thank you so much sir. I look forward to meeting you."

We both hang up and I go in search of my lunch. Usually, Stacy has it delivered to me between 11:30 and noon but its now 12:15pm and I have yet to see it or her, come to think of it. She's still not at her desk. That's strange, I guess Ill go for a walk then. I haven't had a sub in a while, and I love the ones from the deli down the block. I text

Erik to see if he wants one as well, but I don't receive an answer until I'm already on my way back to the office.

Erik
Sorry, it's been a busy morning for me. I ordered in some Thai.

Damon
That would have been good too. Stacy is a-wall today, so I decided to go and get my own food. I'm just in the elevator now, ill stop by your office and we can have lunch together.

Erik
NO!

Sorry, not today, I'm very busy.

Damon
Since when do you care about work? Not saying you slack off, but usually you're the first one to say let's have lunch together.

Erik
I just feel very behind today, so I'm using it to catch up. If I come and have lunch with you, we both know I won't get anything else done today.

Hmm, Erik was acting really weird, and I wasn't sure why, but I stepped off the elevator and back into my office to enjoy my BLT. Stacy still wasn't at her seat; I wonder if she was ill and had gone home for the day. I hope she would have at least told me she was though.

***

At 3pm I see Stacy slide into her desk.
"Stacy, may I see you a minute."
She gets up and walks into the office, her cheeks are flushed, her lipstick is smudged, and her knees are dirty. I choose to ignore all that because I don't need a sexual harassment charge on my hands for noticing things like that and voicing it.
"Close the door and sit down please." I say.
She does as asked "am I in trouble for something sir?"
"I was just wondering if you were feeling ill today? I haven't seen you all day."
"I've been at my desk and helping other people with things all day sir."
She has never lied to me like that before, does she think I'm stupid?
"Do not lie to me, I know that you were gone all day. I saw you when you first showed up because you brought me coffee, and then around 10 when Erik showed up to say good morning to me you disappeared. I thought maybe you went to get him a coffee as well, but it doesn't take 5 hours to get someone a coffee. He also has his own assistant."
"I went and got him a coffee and then I came right back, sir. Alex is out sick today."

"No, you did not. I had to call and set up my own meeting because you weren't here to do it, I also added it to my calendar, and I went and got my own lunch because you didn't have one delivered to me today. I am capable of doing all those things, but I employ you for a reason Stacy. You can not just disappear for majority the day and expect to get paid for it. I don't know what you were doing, and obviously you're not going to enlighten me. You will be paid for half a day today, and that's me being generous. Seeing as you didn't do anything, you are free to go home and come back when your ready to do your job. Consider this a warning Stacy. I hope you feel better. Have a good night."

She stares at me, I've never been this stern with her before, then again, I've never had to. She's never not done her job, but for her to full out lie to my face and say she was at her desk all day when I know she wasn't not okay with me. She gets up and walks out of my office, grabs her coat and purse and heads for the elevator. I hope she is ready to work tomorrow because there's a lot of things we need to catch up on.

Chapter Thirteen:

Olivia

I sit at my desk trying to organize the next charity event when a text comes through. We try to have one every couple months and a lot of work goes into each one.

Damon
Good morning beautiful, would you be free for lunch today? I would love to see you again.

I don't know why he can't just admit that he wants me, we hook up, and go on our separate ways.

Olivia
I can't today sorry, I'm swamped with work.

Damon
No problem, how about supper then? Everyone's got to eat, am I right?

Olivia
You know if I agree to this then it'll count as our second date and ill be done haha!

Damon

Come on, you act all tough but we both know you can't wait to go out with me again. This whole hard to get thing isn't necessary.

Why can't we have more than the two dates? I would love to date you.

Olivia

I'm not playing hard to get, I just don't date. I usually do one-night stands. But you don't seem to want to let me, so here we are.

Damon

Sorry sweetheart, I'm a commitment type of guy. I want it all, the marriage, the kids. Everything, and I have a feeling you're the girl for me.

Oh, of course I would get matched up with a guy like this! This is the type of guy that Chellsea should have gotten. The one that's looking for the whole package deal wrapped up with a pretty bow. I just want sex and a good meal and I'm good. I choose to ignore anything else that comes in from him today. Let's see if that gets though to him or not.

***

I'm home alone tonight, Marina is at the bar working and Chellsea and Aly have their own thing going on. I decide I'm going to have some me time by drinking some well-deserved wine and watching one of my favourite girly movies. Its my little secret, I like to watch romantic dance movies, don't tell anyone, it'll ruin my reputation for being such a hard ass.

About halfway through the movie when the juicy stuff starts to happen I get a text.

Damon
I'm sorry that I scared you off, usually that's the other way around. I just want to get to know you more, your fun to be around. What are you doing tonight?

Olivia
It's fine. I'm currently watching a movie and drinking wine. I'm in comfy mode, no pants.

This is the time for him to show me how he really is. If he doesn't take my bait, there is no hope in a future for us. He won't let us be physical until we go on another date, so we'll see.

Damon
I'm trying to be good and respectful here and then you have to go and tell me you're not wearing any pants? Ugh, why do you do this to me? You have killer legs! I'm sure your ass is great too!

He sort of took the bate, so I'm going to test him a little more by sending him a picture of my legs and a wine glass. Let's see what his comeback will be now.

Olivia
Sent an image.

Damon

Are you trying to kill me? I can't touch you because you won't let me take you out on the second date, so now you're going to torture me?

Olivia
Well, if I had let you take me to dinner we wouldn't be at a house, which means we STILL wouldn't have been able to deal with this sexual tension between us. Now, would we?

Damon

I could come over now. I can bring dinner. Or you could come here? I could send a car…

Olivia
I already ate, I'm having me time at home tonight. All the girls are gone.

Damon

Ok, I get it. We're still playing the hard-to-get game. How did girl's night go the other night?

Olivia
It went well, I'm waiting to hear how her date went.

There's other ways we could work on the sexual tension between us…

Sent an image.

This time I sent him a picture of me from the mouth down wearing my little night shirt. I still have my bright red lipstick on as well, so it really makes my mouth stand out. If he doesn't go for sexting this time, then there's really no hope for us at all.

Damon
Woah, what I wouldn't do to you if I were there right now!

Olivia
Do tell….

Damon
Well, I would start by coming up to you and standing you up, I would look you up and down and then let my hands travel. I would stand behind you and kiss your neck softly well I grabbed your ass. I'm not going to lie, I would likely let out a groan from that, I love your ass!

Olivia
Do continue... you have my attention.

I can feel my head fall back on to your shoulder as a let out a little whimper.

Damon
From behind you I would be able to see down your shirt perfectly. I would slide my hand around and grab your tit. I imagine you would fit perfectly! I'm sure at this point you would be able to feel my hard on through my clothes.

Olivia
Mmm..

I would turn around and kiss you the drop down to my knees and uncage your cock. I would then look up at you as a grabbed a hold and slide it into my mouth.

Damon
Oh, were really doing this hey? Okay.

I want to feel your lips wrapped around my cock, you could be in control, or I could. Whichever you would prefer, I'd be okay with either. Especially if you looked up at me well doing it.

Olivia

I love looking up at a man when I suck on his cock. Then I can watch them loose all their control.
Personally, I love to be in control of the blow job, but I love when they hold my hair back. Do you enjoy that or are you more of a wall grabber?

Damon

Oh Hunny, I'm very vocal when I'm getting head, you will be able to feel exactly how I feel. I also like grabbing a hold of the girl's hair well I do it, makes it more exciting. Not that it doesn't already feel amazing!

I'm playing with myself, are you?

I feel myself starting to lose control and I don't want to cum before you do. I help you up from the floor and get you to lay down on the couch. I take off my shirt and lift yours up so I can get to those amazing tits!

I fist them and bring my mouth down to put one in my mouth, it tastes just how I imagined it would! Amazing!

Olivia
What would happen if I told you, I was?

Damon

I would want to see pictures if I can't be there myself for it. But that might be a little forward of me.

I continue to suck on your nipples and play with one well I bring my other hand down to play with your pussy. I slide your underwear to the side and dip my finger in. Your already wet for me, I slide one in as I put my thumb on your clit.

Olivia

If I sent you a picture, there's a chance I wouldn't get to actually have sex with you. You're just going to have to deal with this until we're together for real…

…. Side note though, I'm totally playing with myself.

Tell me what else you would do. I'm copying what you say so I can image its you doing it.

I run to my bedroom and grab BOB out of the drawer. I slide my underwear off and lay down on my bed. I'm ready to use BOB when he gets to the good parts, but of now my fingers will do.

Damon

Baby, you are a dream come true!

You moan as I slide another finger in and start to pick up the pace.

I take my mouth off of your nipples and pull you out so that you're laying down more and then latch on to your clit with my tongue. I lick you up and down, going between fast and slow.

Matching the speed with how I slide my fingers inside you.

Olivia

I'm close, get to the good stuff.

Are you close?

Damon

Very.

I lick a few more times, twirling it around to make you squirm a bit. Then I get up, pulling you with me and bend you over the couch and slide in.

I pull out of you and smack myself softly on your ass, then I slide back in. I've found my new favourite place to be.

I start slowly at first, letting you get use to me and then i pick up the pace. Trying to keep a steady rhythm as I reach around to grab your tit.

I'm so close, but I'm waiting for you.

Olivia
I just finished.

Why couldn't we actually do this in person?

Damon
I wish I could have heard you cum.

Mmmmm...

*Just thinking about it pushed me over the edge.
I think you need to ask yourself that question
darling.*

Olivia
*Well thanks for helping me get off. I defiantly
needed that tonight. Would have been better
with you then a vibe, but BOB has helped me
though worse times.*

Damon
*You did not just tell me you used a vibrator
called BOB to get you off? I can't wait to use that
on you on day, make you go crazy.*

*Or better yet, watch you get yourself off with
BOB in front of me!*

Olivia
I'll be sure to pack BOB for our second date, you know just in case. ▯

                              Damon
I cannot wait to put that sassy mouth to the test.

I KNOW you did not just try to tell me I wouldn't be able to get your off without BOB!

Olivia
You said it not me!

So far, your 0 and he's 1.

Good night! BOB says thanks for the assistance.

                              Damon
                    No no no, I don't think so.

BOB assisted me; I DIDN'T assist him.

Olivia
Sure sure, good night.

Busy day tomorrow.

Damon

This isn't over.

Have a good sleep.

Try to think of me 🙂

Yawning I made my way into the kitchen the next morning, filling up for a fresh pot of coffee and to hear about Chelsea's date. Mine had gone well, better then my most recent dates and Damon has been relentless with texting and emailing me for a second date. Despite my efforts I could not hold back the smile splitting my face.

"What has you all in smiles?" Marina walks into the kitchen grabbing her mug from the cupboard. I shrugged as she passed me my mug "just had a really good sleep and I am excited to hear about Chelsea's date." I could tell Marina did not believe me, but I was not ready to tell her that I had agreed to a second date with Damon.

I walked over to the shared door to our suits and opened it "ladies, coffee is ready!" Chellsea sulks into the living room making her way to the kitchen pouring herself a cup of coffee. Aly walks in after her and we lock eyes. She shrugs and mouths "rough date." I nod knowing this was going to be a long story, we may need more coffee.

"It was horrible" Chellsea wailed with her face in her hands. I feel for her honestly, between the two of us she wants to fall in love more then anyone else. She deserves it, Chellsea is sweet and bubbly, I wont lie my heart is breaking for her a little bit. Chellsea recited the events of her night, rough was an understatement. Tonight, will be another girls night, ill be sure to stock up on our favourite ice creams.

"He took me to a dive bar and told me I was paying because he had already paid for the date. This made sense on the text I received from her last night if there was a time limit on the date. I told her no, that it was frowned upon, but I will be sending an email to the higher ups about what had happened to Chellsea, so she didn't get penalized at work.

This dirt bag told Chellsea that because he paid for her that he expected her to bang him at the end of the night. I sat staring at my coffee no longer warm wondering if there was any way I can track this guy down and teach him some manners. No women should ever be treated like this.

"I can show you what a real date looks like Chels" Aly smirked. For the first time in the morning Chellsea laughed and smiled. Things we back to normal.

At least they were until Marina saw my phone buzz from a text from Damon.

Damon
Can't wait for next weekend.

"What's this?!" Marina squealed holding up my phone for everyone to see. There was a collective gasp, genuine, as Olivia Harper doesn't do second dates. So much for going back to normal. Before I could get bombarded with questions there was a knock on the door. "I'll get it!" I rushed to the front door before anyone could protest.

"Why good morning!" Xander stood in the doorway with a grin on his face.

Aly rolled her eyes "Xander this is our time, what are you doing here?" She tried to sound serious but truthfully, she always loved seeing my brother. Xander placed a hand on his heart with mock hurt on his face "I just wanted to see my beautiful sister and her friends before I headed out of town for a work conference." I side stepped to let him in and made my way back to the table.

I peeked over to Marina who was sheepishly looking down at her coffee mug, I smiled to myself.

"You can come sit here Xander" I patted the now empty chair between me and Marina.

She looked up at me in horror with her bright eyes. I responded with a shrug.

"Don't mind if I do" Xander sauntered over and gave Marina a wink. "What's new and exciting with you Mar?"

She took a moment to collect herself and smiled "Not much, you know, surviving" She gave an awkward laugh. Chellsea intervened, sliding a mug towards Xander filled with fresh coffee.

"We were just talking about how Liv here is going on a second date with the Rich douche" I knew Marina wouldn't just let this go, I shot her a glare.

Xander nearly choked on his coffee "What? You haven't gone on a second date in years! Are you feeling, ok? Do you need a doctor?" Xander placed his hand on my forehead "Quick how many fingers am I holding up?" he put up two fingers for me to count. I flipped him off as a response. He leaned back in his chair and exhaled "Ok, good you're obviously fine. Same Ol' Liv" he turned his attention back to Marina who has found her coffee mug to be so interesting every time he looked at her.

Marina and Xander were pretty close in age, he was barely a year older than her but always took a liking to her since we were kids, I had a suspicion that maybe he would ask her out if her and her boyfriend ever broke up. He never had the chance before she started dating Aaron, maybe he's oblivious to the signs she gives off when he's around, but then again, he doesn't know her any other way. Those two should be together, they have more chemistry than Marina and Aaron ever have.

"So, what makes this guy so special to earn a second date?" Aly keeping the focus back to me.

I shrugged "he offered to double his donation, so I'm really doing it for the kids."

When they realized that's about all they were going to get from me the topic dropped. We sat together chatting with Xander about his upcoming trip, when no one was looking I quickly sent Damon a reply.

Olivia
Don't get too excited, I'm doing this for the kids…

But I'm looking forward to seeing the laid-back Damon.

Xander was getting ready to head out "Are we still good for dinner on Thursday?" He asks while he put on his jacket.
I smiled "Oh it's your birthday again? Didn't we celebrate last year"
Xander rolled his eyes at me and laughed "Yeah that's how birthdays work, they come every year"
"Of course, I'll meet you at moms."

Chapter Fourteen:
Damon

What on earth am I going to do with this girl? Out of nowhere she wanted to sext and then she started sending me nonrevealing, revealing pictures. Even though I came, my dick still hasn't softened, it doesn't want my hand, it wants to be wrapped up in her warm pussy.

And then she went and told me that she was masturbating and using a vibrator to boot! I've never met a woman that is so in tune with her sexuality. One way or another I'm going to get her to fall for me though, this is going to happen. She just doesn't know it yet.

***

The next morning, I get up and have to take care of myself for the millionth time, no matter what I can't stop thinking about her and every time I do I get a hard on. Its like I'm a teenage boy all over again! I decide to hop in the shower but even that does help, I just start thinking of how I wish she was here, and I could rub soap all over her sexy body and then fuck her well she's covered in bubbles. I come out of my daydream to notice that my hand is around my cock and I'm close, so I continue with my daydream and get to release.

***

I sit at my desk looking at my computer, my assistant, Stacy, had just brought me a coffee refill. I'm researching the background for this guy that's coming in for a talk soon. Tristan Callaghan, he is from old money and seems to be a big daddy's boy. He's everywhere that he is, its like they're attached at the hip, I wouldn't be surprised if he showed up with his father. I have the meeting with him in a few days and until then I have time to find out everything I can about him to see if it's something I'd be interested in investing in. A lot of people come to me to help them start a business because they don't have the backing to do it themselves.

There is a knock on my door "Excuse me, Mr. Thompson. There is a Mr. Harper here to see you. Stacy says.

Harper? That's Olivia's last name "I wasn't expecting anyone today, does he have a first name?" I asked.

"Ahh…" she looks over her shoulder at Mr. Harper I'm assuming.

I hear a deep voice answer "Xander, miss", I recognize it immediately.

"He can come in, I know him. Thank you, Stacy." Xander walks into my office in a stylish suit, not as expensive as mine is I'm sure, but it looks good on him and that's what matters. "Have a seat, sorry I wasn't expecting you. Are you looking to have me invest in something?"

He sits down "No, actually I am here as a silent favor to Olivia. You see, she has been hurt in the past, I'm not sure if you are aware of this or not. But she has, and since we lost our dad, I'm here to give you the 'you better respect my girl talk.'"

I swallow and stare at him, wanting to make sure he's serious. Does he really think I would do something to harm Olivia? I would never, I want to hang the moon for her. "Oh, that's sweet of you. You don't need to worry about her with me though."

"I worry about her with everyone she decides to get with. Are you aware that you are only the second person she has agreed to go on a second date with since Tristan? What an asshole he turned out to be!"

Tristan, it can't be the same one can it? No way, just a coincidence that he has the same name really.

"I did actually. She just wanted to hook up and be done with me. That's not how I work unfortunately, so I'm fighting for her, I am prepared to gravel if needed."

"Good, that's very good. Another way to separate you from that asshole. Has she told you what he did to her? Probably not." I shake my head. "Well, they were set up by our fathers. They were friends you see, how I have no idea. But they were and one day they decided that they were going to set up a date for them. And then they were pushed together at every function, and they ended up just becoming an item. Her father thought they were good people; I don't think he would say that now after what happened. He just wanted Olivia to be happy, personally I think that the last weekend they spent up at the cabin, he said so. He told her to stay with him and give him a chance, so she did because she loved him very much. They had a very close relationship. Anyways, I'm getting sidetracked, they were due to get married, he had just proposed to her, and they went to announce it to his parents. Both his parents told her that it wasn't allowed, they forbid it. So, he broke up with her and asked for the ring back. He still tries to get a hold of her to hook up, but thankfully she turns him down every time. He was very forceful, and unfair in their relationship, he even tried to force himself upon her. The weekend before Olivia and our dad went up to the cabin for the weekend before her died. She didn't want to break our fathers wishes, so she stayed with him, didn't even tell our dad that he had tried to force her. That is the reason that she doesn't do second dates now, she is scared to get close to someone and they do what that asshole did to her."

That is a lot to process, wow! I understand her hard shell that she walks around carrying now, I can't believe she stayed with him just because her dad wanted her to. Xander just said that he wanted her to be happy, she wasn't happy. So, I don't think that's what he was wanting.

"Thank you for telling me that, I don't know if she ever would have herself. She only told me that she doesn't do second dates and I thought it was a way of playing hard to get. Its hard to hear about your father passing too."

"Thank you, it was hard on us when he died so suddenly, none of us even knew he was sick, he chose to hide it from all of us and suffer alone. I guess it was his way of making sure she didn't change the way they treated him. Didn't want anyone to treat him like he was sick." He looks away from me for a second. "Back to why I'm here though, if you hurt her, you won't have to deal with her, you'll be dealing with me, and her four best friends. So, keep that in mind, you don't want to piss us off! I wish you a good day."

We shake hands and he leaves, well that was an interesting start to my morning. As Xander was leaving I stopped him "One more thing before you go"

"Yeah?" Xander turned back to me.

"What's Tristan's last name?" I asked

He tilted his head for a moment "You're not going to kill him, are you?"

I shook my head.

"Ok good. Its Callaghan" He said and walked out.

"YOU HAVE GOT TO BE FUCKING KIDDING ME!" I scream, and slam my fist against the desk, sending some of my papers flying.

Stacy and Eric rush into my office, Erik has a bit of smeared lipstick on his face and Stacy's lipstick is smeared. Interesting...

"What? What happened? Are you okay? Did something happen? TELL ME!!!" Erik screams back at me.

I stare at him. "I would if you would shut up for a minute! You know that Tristan guy that reached out to me to invest in his company? The one I have a meeting with on Friday..."

"Yes" they say in unison.

"Well, turns out that is Olivia's Tristan. The one that mistreated her and made her so fragile, yet strong. Ugh, I don't want to meet with this guy!" I slam my fist against the desk again.

"Umm... I'm going to go get your guys some lunch. It sounds like you need to talk." Stacy says as she exits the office after grabbing her coat.

I turn back to Erik to see him staring after her, "umm... are you sleeping with my assistant?"

"What? Why would you ask that?"

"Well for one you have lipstick on your face, and hers was smudged. Secondly, you both got here at the same time. If you weren't together, she should have been here first because she works outside my office AS MY ASSISTANT, might I add again. In case that didn't clue in for you.

"No, were not sleeping together, I may have kissed her once. But that's all that happened, now back to this asshat. Do you know what he wants to meet with you about?"

I shake my head "No, I don't even know if he knows who I am. I feel like an idiot, I've been looking at pictures of him and his family all morning and it didn't clue into me that he was that asshole from the auction. How did I not recognize it?"

"Now, now, don't beat yourself up about it. I, being the older brother would like to give you some advice here." I stare at him bewildered, this is always his go to when he thinks I need advice, this time I do so ill go with it. He's older by a whole 2 minutes though, I wouldn't really say he's my older brother. "Why don't you continue to meet with him, see if he actually has a good idea and then if he does take it to another company instead. Rub it in his face that you're not going to sit here and help him after he hurt your woman."

"Hmmm… that's actually a good idea. I like it, okay ill do that. On a side note, we have to talk about you and Stacy further. You are not supposed to be hooking up with people in the office, you know better than that."

"Gotta go, sorry. Lots to do. It was nice talking to you. Enjoy your lunch when Stacy gets back!" And then he hightails it out of my office, ugh, I wish he would stop being such a playboy and settle down already. If he didn't look exactly like me, except for that dimple when he smiles, it wouldn't bug me so much. However, I get pegged as a playboy.

I haven't heard from Olivia all day, so I decide to message her and see if her day is better then mine.

Chapter Fifteen:
Olivia

Damon

Hey beautiful, how is your day going so far?

How did Chellsea's date go?

Olivia

I'm pretty good, I have to go to the store when I'm done work for the day. I don't feel like shopping today, but I've got to.

Chellsea's date was a dud, he tried to tell her that because he paid so much for the date that she needed to pay for the meal and that he expected her to put out. She climbed out of the window; I feel so bad for her.

Damon

WHAT?! That's uncalled for on so many levels. Some men are such scum, I'm sorry that happened to her.

Why are you going to the store?

Olivia

I need to load up on ice cream. Whenever one of us goes through a breakup or a bad date we get together and pig out on ice cream. Well slamming the men that have hurt us in the past, drink wine and watch sappy movies wishing that was the man we had gone out with instead.

Damon

That sounds both healthy and not haha!

Romance movies seem to give woman an unrealistic hope for relationships. I try my best to live up to them, but even I can't compare to that.

What kind of ice cream do you and the girls like?

Olivia

My favourite is mint chocolate chunk. Marina's is Neapolitan. Chellsea's is cookies and cream. And Aly's is anything involving cheesecake. If they don't end up having one of our flavours, we just get a giant tub of chocolate and put sprinkles on it haha!

Damon

Those are good flavour choices. I'm gad you have such a great relationship with your girls!

Olivia

Me too! I wouldn't be anywhere without them. They're my rock.

Damon

My brother Erik is like that for me. I'm not close with many people but I am close to my brother.

Its nearing 5pm and I'm almost done for the day. I'm just about to get up to get Chellsea so that we can head to the store on our way home when she walks over to me with a gift basket in her hands and a huge smile on her face.

"I was just coming to get you. What's this? It looks super familiar." I ask her.

"You would be correct; this is from Damon. He really is so sweet. We have to get home quickly, otherwise the ice cream is going to melt."

"Did you just say ice cream?" We head down to the parkade to make our way home.

"Yes. I already opened it, because I wasn't sure who it was from. I thought maybe it was from the douche from last night sending me an apology, but then I figured after the way he acted he wouldn't send something like this. Anyways, I'm babbling. Damon sent a pint of ice cream for each of us, a couple bottles of wine and a few sappy movies. Its like he knew exactly what we like, is he a mind reader?"

"He's so smooth. I was talking to him earlier about how we were getting together tonight to have another girl's night because of your dud of a date last night. I also told him what we do and that I was having issues getting motivation to go to the store after work. So, I guess he solved that problem for me. I guess this means I might actually have to give him a chance, he's the opposite of Tristan."

When we get home, I dig through it to see what he sent. He listened to everything I said, there is one of each of our favorite ice creams in here, as well as another three bottles of wine from the last basket. We already have the movies he sent but it's the thought that counts, and at least he guessed right. Then I find the note, with a certificate attached for any restaurant of our choosing to deliver to us on him.

Don't let this get to you. You are a smart, strong woman that deserves to be pampered. Keep looking until you find the right one. -Damon.
P.S – Thanks for putting in a good word to Olivia for me.

I send off a quick message to Damon after putting the ice cream in the freezer.

Olivia
Thank you for helping put a smile on Chellsea's face today, she really needed that.

Damon
You're welcome.

Olivia
The note was really sweet too.

Damon

I wanted to make sure she knew that not all men are like that.

Did you decide what you're having for supper tonight?

Olivia

No, not yet. I'll let her decide since it's her night. But we typically go for junk food on nights like this, its comfort for the soul.

Damon

Well enjoy whatever you decide on.

I won't keep you, have a great night. Go cheer your friend up.

I was a little early as I walked up to my mom's front door knocked and opened the door.
"Hey ma, I'm here"
"I'm in the kitchen sweetie" Mom called out
It smelled fantastic, mom was making her slow cooked roast, I peeked in the oven and my mouth started to water seeing her potato au gratin.
"I am starving" I said closing the oven. Mom was icing Xander's cake, I gave her a side hug to steal a taste of frosting.
She slapped my hand away "Go on now, you can wait like the rest of us."

I frowned "but mom, I thought I was the favourite! Don't I get special treatment?"

She chuckled "I love both my children equally, don't give me that. Although with today being your brother's birthday, he might get some extra love and special treatment" she winked at me.

I slid onto the bar stool at the island and watched her finish icing the cake.

I always loved the way mom would make cakes; she was so good at it. I tried my best, but I could never make anything as good as she did. Some say that's because you always crave your mothers cooking. It's the feeling involved in it I think.

"So, mom. Do you have any exciting news to share with me?"

She looks up at me "like what?"

"I dunno, just news you know? Did you get a new friend, hook up with someone, start seeing someone, get a new phone. Just something, anything. Tell me something new and exciting that's happened to you since we last talked."

She pondered that a minute "Well, first of all I already had my happy ending, I can't get that lucky twice. So, you can stop asking me about dating and hooking up. But nothing really exciting has happened to me, me and Julie went for drinks the other night."

"Come on mom, we all miss dad. But he would want you to be happy and find someone else that helps you get there."

"I don't need a man sweetie, I have you and your brother to keep me company." She comes around and kissed my temple just as Xander walks in the house.

"Hey mom. Hey sis. how's it going? Is that my cake? It looks great mom! And supper smells amazing!" He says as he waltzes into the kitchen and gives us both a quick hug.

"Xander, I was just telling mom that she needs to put herself out there and be open to meeting another man. Dad would want her to be happy, don't you agree" I say with a smirk.

"Well of course I think that. But your one to talk misses fuck and done."

"Hey, I told you that was a secret. Moms not supposed to know that!" I look from Xander to my mom. She's not shocked though.

"Sweetie, I've been there before, I know what a one-night stand is. I also know that your libido is liking going crazy, so get whatever sex you can when you can." She winks at me.

"MOM!" Both me and Xander scream at her.

"What? I'm human too! Dinners ready, lets set the table."

Xander grab the plates, utensils and wine glasses, I take a dish with me as well as a bottle of wine, open it and pour some into each glass. When the table is set, we sit down and start eating.

"You know you two I'm not getting any younger, I want grandkids one day!"

I choked on my wine "Yeah no, not from me, Xander better find a girl and settle down."

Xander leaned back in his chair "You're closer than me in that world, mom did you know she is going on a second date."

"Olivia! You're going on a second date?" mom gasped at me.

I glared at Xander "Why is my dating life such a hot topic for everyone! This is for charity."

Mom sighed "Olivia you are killing me, what's wrong with this one?"

"Well...um...nothing actually" I stuttered trying to think of a reason not to date him.

"He's actually pretty decent mom" Xander added his two cents.

"How would you know? The only interaction you have had was bidding against him at the auction." I eyed him.

"You bid for your own sister for a date?" mom added. "Should I be concerned?" She eyed him up.

"I didn't want Tristan to win the date" He shrugged.

Mom scoffed at Tristan's name. "I never liked that boy." She shook her head. "If your dad knew how he was acting he would have punched him in the nose."

I laughed because I knew she was right. "Yeah, dad was no bull-shit that's for sure."

Mom smacked my arm "Watch your mouth young lady."

I shrugged and took a sip of wine.

"Remember when dad got into 'words' with the neighbour down the street when his son took my bike?" Xander laughed.

"That poor man went ghost white and brought little Johnny over with your bike cleaned and polished." Mom's smile warmed my heart.

"Dad had a heart of gold, but he never shied away from speaking his mind." That is something I was proud to have inherited from him.

Mom sighed. "I miss going to the cabin with him and you kids. We were forever outside either down by the lake or hiking through the forest."

"We used to spend the whole summer out there, dad would commute an hour back into town for work, come back and we would just stay out at the cabin."

"Don't forget the fishing!" I added

"If you can't catch your dinner, then you're not eating.'" We all said in unison and laughed.

"What about the time he went out to the island on the salmon excursion for two weeks and filled the deep freezer."

Mom rolled her eyes "It took a solid year to get through all of that."

"I think dad would like Damon actually," Xander said, pushing his food on his plate refusing to make eye contact with me.

I was glaring daggers at him "How do you know that? Must I reiterate you only SAW him at the charity event?"

Xander shifted in his seat, he was keeping something from me.

"And I went to his office and talked to him." Xander looked at me.

"You what?!" I gasped.

"Oh, tell me, tell me, tell me!" Mom put her chin on her hands.

He shrugged "I wanted to give him the you better treat her right speech"

I sat there in shock waiting for him to continue. Xander flashed me a huge smile "I like him, he was polite and I'm pretty sure he would destroy Tristan if he ever got the chance, he actually seems like a stand-up guy."

"Oh sweetie, he sounds amazing! I can't wait to meet him" Mom patted my arm.

I groaned and put my face in my hands "No mom, this is not turning into a relationship. I just agreed for a second date because he offered to double his donation to the Children's hospital."

"Don't give me that bullshit Olivia Harper, money has never been a motive for you." She points her finger at me.

"But I..."

"No but! I have heard it all and you can't fool me, you obviously see something in this young man otherwise you wouldn't agree to go on a date with him."

I didn't respond.

"Just give him an actual chance sweetie it's all I ask."

I deflated "I'm going on a second date! Isn't that enough?"

"Not if you don't actually try" she added.

I nodded in agreement and finished my wine.

I always loved coming to my mother's house, whether it was just to visit or to eat dinner. One thing we kept up after dad died was that we always got together for each others' birthdays, no matter what. When we do eventually end up setting down, I imagine we'll just add them to the mix. But for right now I love our time together. Plus, like a said, Xander better meet a woman and start popping out those grand babies for mom, because its not coming from me anytime soon, or ever!

Before I knew it the night was over, and we were saying our goodbyes.

"Come on sis, I'll walk you to your car. Goodbye mom. Thank you for a lovely birthday." He kissed her cheek and gave her a hug. I did the same and we were off.

"Why didn't you tell me you were going to confront Damon? What makes you even think you had to?" I ask Xander.

"That day before I went on my business trip I found out where he worked and decided to pop in and see him. You won't admit it but I know your starting to fall for this guy, so I had to make sure he wasn't another Tristan. You'll be glad to hear I approve, it doesn't mean I want to hear any sex stories though, that would be weird. "

"And going to tell this guy I'm 'dating'" I hold up my hands and quote the word dating "isn't weird?"

"No, its not. I silently promised dad I would look after you, this is one way of doing that."

"Ok, well thank you, I guess."

"Anytime sis." He gave me a hug and kissed my temple.

"Happy birthday Xander, thank you for always being there for me when I need you."
He smiled at me, and I got in my car. I wasn't ready to admit to anyone yet that I was indeed starting to fall for Damon, that was going to be my little secret.

Chapter Sixteen:
Damon

I went digging though my recipe book, I knew what I wanted to make her, and I knew how to make it, I've made it so many times. Its my favourite dish, but I didn't want to make it wrong for her and her end up hating it. So, I found the recipe for Chicken Florentine Pasta and started to take note of what I needed from the store. The only thing I had here was garlic, so I headed to the store, after switching my clothes.

Chicken Florentine Pasta
Feeds 2-3
1 TBSP – Garlic Butter (Butter works too)
¼ - red onion
4 strips bacon – cut into pieces
2 cups – spinach
1 TSP – garlic
16 oz – fettuccine noodles
1 – chicken breast Cooked and cut up)
2 Cups - Cream sauce (you can buy some or make your own)
2 TBSP – Whipping Cream

Most people would assume that I wouldn't be so mundane as to go to the grocery store myself being a billionaire and all, but I thought it was a great time to spend some quality time with yourself. I love shopping, even if its for something as simple as grocery's. Plus, it makes the dinner more special if I do it myself.

"Hello Mr. Thomson. How are you today?" Rebecca the store clerk greets me as I walk in.

"I'm well Becky, thank you for asking. How are you? Also, how many times do I have to tell you to call me Damon?" I say as I walk over to her.

"I'm great thanks! Charlie just turned 5 this week, he loved that toy you sent for him. You really didn't have to do that you know."

"I know I didn't, but I wanted to. What's the point of having money if you can't spend it on people? I'm glad he liked it. Anyway, I'm off to do some shopping, I have a date tomorrow that I need to prep for. I'll see you in a bit."

I grab a cart and start in the bread aisle, the one thing I don't make from scratch is garlic bread, I'm a sucker for the store-bought ones, you know the ones you find in a tin foil pack that you cook in the oven for 40 minutes and it comes out perfectly crispy and ready to eat? I've tried to make it myself but its not the same, so I just buy it instead. Me and Erik use to love this dish too, he wouldn't know how to make it if I showed him though. I tried once and he nearly burnt down my house! Never again have I tried to teach that man how to cook, he's content living off of takeout and homemade meals that others make for him, so that's good enough for me.

Me on the other hand, have always loved cooking. There's just something about it that speaks to me, I'm not going to say I'm the best cook around, but I do know how to make quite a bit of things. I hired a chef for a few months to teach me how to up my cooking skills as well, it was a lot of fun.

Next, I find the onions and spinach and add those to my cart. Then I make my way to the meat department and pick up a package of chicken and bacon. One thing I enjoy about this dish is that it has so many flavours in it, I could literally eat it every day.

I head to the dry goods section and grab a couple cans of Alfredo sauce, and a box of fettuccine noodles. Next, I head to the dairy section and grab a jug of milk, cream and some parmesan cheese.

As I'm making my way to the front counter, I spot a beautiful bouquet of roses and decide to add those to my cart as well, they will make a nice centrepiece for my table. I pay for my purchase and then head back home to start prepping what I can for the meal.

I put the flowers into a vase and set them on the table, wash my hands and get to work on dicing up the onion and bacon. I place them each into their own containers and set them in the fridge. Next, I set up a pot to boil the noodles needed, so that I can cool them and just heat them up in the microwave quick before adding them to the pan.

I add some oil to a pan and wait for it to heat up before I add the seasoned chicken breast to it to cook up. I'm trying to be as prepared as I can for tomorrow so that I have more time with her instead of cooking. The pasta water just started boiling as well so I quickly grab the noodles and add them in, then set a timer for 8 minutes.

Last thing I have to make is the cream sauce, I like to make it well the other things are cooking so that I can watch them all at once. Another reason this dish is easier to prep for the day before is because you end up with a lot of dishes at the end of it.

I start by placing some butter into a pan and letting it melt. Once its melted you add a little bit of flour to thicken it up. I flip the chicken over and then add the milk, cream, garlic, parmesan, salt, pepper and sugar to the cream sauce. Let that come to a simmer and then add in the Alfredo sauce, once that reaches a boil your good to go, so I turn off the heat and pour it into a container to cool down. The chicken and pasta is done already and ready for me to put away. I put the pasta into a container, chop of the chicken and place both in the fridge. While I wait for the sauce to cool down, I decide to crack a beer and call my mother.

"Damon my love, how are you?" Mom was always happy to hear from me.
"I'm great, been getting a plan together for a date coming up"

"Oh, a date? She must be special, when was the last time you went out with a nice girl"

"Well actually a few weeks ago with the same girl, this is our second date"

I swore I could hear her smile through the phone

"Are you taking her somewhere special?"

"Well, that's what I'm struggling with right now, I took her to the aquarium went all flashy, but she wants to see my down to earth side."

"Oh Damon, don't over think this! Just be true to yourself and you cannot fail"

"You're my mom, your supposed to say that kind of thing."

"Oh hush, when have I ever said something, I didn't believe about my boys?"

I let out a laugh "Mom, you lie about Erik all the time."

"Well, that's different, I'm not proud of the fact that he sleeps around. I love your brother, but I wish he would stop that, find a nice girl and settle down."

"You and me both mom, you and me both. I'm not sure we're ever going to see that though, so I wouldn't hold your breath."

"Don't say that now. Eventually a girl will come along and sweep him off his feet. She'll have to be a strong one though, none of this falling to her knees for him stuff or he'll walk all over her."

"So true mom. I hope the day comes soon. How's dad?"

"Oh, he's good sweetie. He's watching the game right now, I think. What game I couldn't tell you, you know I don't care for that sort of thing."

"Well, that's good to hear. Anyways mom, I'm going to let you go. I still have some things to set up before the date tomorrow."

"Okay son, you treat her well. I love you; we'll talk soon."

"Love you too mom" I get off the phone and look over at Jack.

"What do you think buddy? Where should I take Olivia?" he lifted his head for a moment, turned around and fell asleep.

"You're no help" I muttered.

How am I not supposed to over think this? This is my last chance to show Olivia I am a decent guy.

I thought back to some of my favourite places to go and unwind. Suddenly it hit me, I should take her to the amusement part by the pier! I can't believe this wasn't my first thought, no pressure, games and rides. I checked the weather for the next few days Saturday should be sunny, but it's supposed to be rain for the rest of the week.

I thought about how amazing it would be to wake up next to her too chilly outside to do anything and stay in bed all morning with coffee, granted if she wants to stay the night. I decided to shoot her off a text.

Damon
Are you free tomorrow for our date?

Olivia

That actually works for me.
I was surprised she didn't try to bail again.

Damon
Great! I will pick you up around 1.

Olivia
That's okay I can meet you there where are we going?

Damon
You won't let me surprise you, will you?

Olivia
Nope, no surprises I need to know what to wear.

I sighed; she is so difficult.

Damon
I was thinking about taking you to the amusement park on the pier, and dinner at my place after?

Olivia
That actually sounds fun, will there be dessert? ⍰

Damon
There will always be dessert my dear.

That went better than I thought, I smiled to myself; it's all or nothing now. I should probably arrange to have some actual dessert as well though. Only one place to go for that.

"Come on boy" I say to Jack as I stand up, hook him up to his leash, grab my jacket and head out the door.

We walk down a few blocks to my favourite bakery. I tie Jack to the pole outside and walk in the door.

"Oh, Mr. Thomson. How are you today? Your out late." Ronnie the store clerk says.

"I know, last minute date tomorrow, you know how it is, I'm sure. I'm well thank you. How are you and the Mrs.?"

"We're good, very good sir. Thank you for asking. What can I get you today?"

"Hmm. I'm not sure what she likes to eat yet. But chocolate is usually a pretty good shot, so give me a variety of some items you would recommend. I trust everything you make."

He adds a few different things to a box and rings me up.

"I've included a card inside so that you know what everything is sir. Just be sure to keep them in your fridge and you'll be fine. I hope you have a great night." He hands me my bag; I thank him and make my way back out to Jack and we begin our walk home.

Chapter Seventeen:

Olivia

I haven't been on a second date since Tristan, I shuddered at the thought of him. It's for the kids I remind myself but every time I say it, I believe in myself a little less. I am getting feelings for Damon; I need to nip this in the bud before I get hurt. Everyone seems to want me to 'give him a chance' and I'm sick of it this is my life is it not? I put on my skinny jeans and a tight white tee, feelings or not, I am going to get what I want at the end of the night. I threw my hair in braids. He said he is taking me to the amusement park, I am excited for that. I sighed maybe getting feelings wouldn't be such a bad idea. He shared so much with me on our first date, he was vulnerable and the fact that he didn't take me home and fuck my brains out after, well that's a first. There was a knock on my door "come in!" I called; Marina entered my room. Maybe it's because we have been friends for so long or maybe I am that easy to read, but Marina saw my conflict before I could say anything.

20 years ago

I sat on the front steps of my house pouting. Xander and his friend Zach got to go to the park by themselves, but I wasn't allowed to go, boys are stupid I thought to myself.

"Liv would you like some ice-cream?" My mom popped her head out the door.

"No, I want to go to the park" I huffed back, I did want ice cream, but I thought if I pouted mom would realize she was being mean and would let me run to the park with Xander and Zach.

Instead, mom sighed "I'm sorry Hunny you can't go to the park alone and I'm busy getting dinner going for grandma and grandpas visit. But I know the new neighbors are moving in today, I heard they have a little girl around your age you can play with."

I wasn't happy with her answer, I turned away and went back to pouting. Mom went back inside, and I waited for Xander to come home, maybe I could force him to dress up in a princess dress again and play tea party with me, he always did.

"Why are you upset?" I didn't realize that a moving truck had pulled in next door. A girl who looked a little older than me had freckles on her face and her brown hair in braids.

"My stupid brother and his stupid friend left me to go play at the park. My mom said I'm not allowed to go without an adult" I frowned.

"Well boys ARE stupid, AND they have cooties" She sat down next to me.

That made me smile. "Yeah, they do but cooties are better than having no one to play with."

"I'll play with you! All my toys are in boxes though." She pointed at the truck as her parents carried boxes into the house.
"We can play with mine!" I squealed. We ran to her parents and asked for permission to have my new friend come play at my house. When they agreed we ran off to my room to play with my dolls.
"My name is Marina by the way" She said brushing my favorite dolls hair.
"I'm Olivia" I smiled at her.

"Liv honestly, not every guy is a douche like Tristan why don't you give this guy a chance?" She said firmly.

I sighed there is the second chance talk again "I am going on a second date with him doesn't that count?"

Marina scoffed "No, it doesn't because you only agreed to go on a second date with this guy because he offered to double his donation to the charity."

I rolled my eyes at her "You know I don't do second dates Mar" She was shaking her head I knew she wouldn't agree with me regardless. I don't want to get hurt again, I was shattered into a million pieces after Tristan, and she was the one who was there helping me put myself together again.

Three years ago

I was so excited to finally announce our engagement to Tristan's family. I was practically bouncing in my seat in the back of the town car, peppering Tristan in kisses and admiring my ring that I was finally allowed to wear in public.

"Settle down your basically vibrating" Tristan laughed. He was smiling but I could tell he was nervous as the smile didn't quite reach his eyes. I pushed the worry aside and took a deep breath and sat back in my seat for the rest of the ride. When we arrived, the servants were waiting for us to help with anything we needed. I was not used to this even after being with Tristan for so long, having people dote on my hand and foot was a strange concept to me and I rather do things myself if I can. Tristan's parents Bryan and Susan waited for us in the solarium with afternoon tea. I flattened out the wrinkles in my dress and made sure my hair was nice and neat back in my headband. I had the biggest smile on my face walking behind Tristan as we made our way to the solarium. "Mom, Dad I have some news, Livvy and I are getting married."

Susan's teacup slipped from her hands and shattered on the ground "Heavens no, this is unacceptable! Bryan tell them they can't!" The maid rushed to the mess carefully cleaning up the shattered glass on the floor. I didn't know what to say they had known me for the past seven years, I have always been so polite and kind to them. I felt like I couldn't breathe, I truly thought they would be happy.

"Son, we need to speak to you" Bryan said pointing a look at me "In private" he added. Tristan nodded and turned to me "Go to the gardens, I will meet you there when I'm done." Slowly I walked to the garden, my feet feeling like led, why didn't he defend in there? I walked around the garden for half an hour waiting for Tristan to return to me. I sat down at the fountain and stared blankly at it.

"Livvy." Tristan said behind me. He walked around and stood in front of me. I fought to hold my tears back scared for what he was going to say.

"Is everything going to be alright?"

"There is a car ready to take you home."

"What!? What do you mean? Are you coming with me?" I'm not able to hold back my tears anymore as they start to flow down my cheeks and my voice shakes.

"No" he replied.

"What why?"

"We can't be together any more Livvy, my parents don't approve of our engagement or our relationship."

"How can that be? We have been together for the past seven years they always loved me." Tristan shook his head and held out his hand to help me up I took it and rose with shaking hands.

"You don't come from money Livvy, my world and your world are different places... you don't belong with me here. They were willing to overlook it until now because they thought we

were just having fun and that I would get you out of my system."
The tears started to fall harder "No! You can't believe that Tristan!" I yelled "We have been through so much together!"
"I do, we are done, stop making a scene."
Tristan was getting impatient with me. I turned and started to walk away towards the front of the house where the car waited for me.
"Livvy wait!" Tristan called out for me.
I turned around hopeful he realized this was a mistake.
"I need my ring back" he held out his hand.
I threw it at his face and never looked back.
The memory still left a bitter taste in my mouth, I had loved him unconditionally, I was faithful, and I was left broken. Even to this day Tristan tries to get into my pants 'why not keep having the fun without the commitment?' Double standard I know, considering how I 'date', but Tristan is trash, ugh I could spit in his face.

"Earth to Liv" Marina snapped her fingers at me, I shook myself from the memory and smiled. "This counts as giving him a chance, I will try" I reassured her, but I doubt nothing Damon could do would change my mind. My phone buzzed next to Marina she picked it up, "He wants to know if you're sure he can't pick you up?" She smiled way too big for my liking.
"Yeah, no that is not happening at all, text him that I will meet him there."

"See you in 10 at my place need my address?" she said out loud. I looked at her mortified

"I said no!" I shouted.

"Too late he said he remembers where you live, he will text you when he is close."

I let go of my breath in relief I could work with that I had him drop me off a block away last weekend I will just cut through the bike path and meet him there. I snatched my phone from Marina's hand.

"That's enough from you cupid" I stuck my tongue out at her.

She rolled her eyes at me "Don't that's enough me, you need to be the one to stop. You don't need to keep closing yourself off from relationships."

"You're starting to sound like Chellsea." I checked my phone Damon was 10 minutes away. I slipped my red leather jacket on and smiled at Marina "I am going on a second date after all." I left her behind.

I quickly walked to the next block and waited at the bike path for Damon to pick me up. I ran up the stairs of the house he had dropped me off at and sat down. When his car pulled up, he stepped out holding the door open for me, then walked over to the steps to help me up and guide me to the car.

"You can pull off any look and still look absolutely stunning Livvy" Damon said with his sexy smile.

"Don't call me Livvy. Olivia or Liv but never Livvy," I glared daggers at him. We are not off to a good start. "I don't need you to wait on me either, I am perfectly capable of standing and walking by myself!" I snapped at him; I knew he was only trying to be a gentleman but his Livvy comment through me off. I know he didn't do it on purpose, but I was instantly transported back into my life with Tristan, which is NOT where I wanted to be.

Damon was shocked at my response but quickly regained his composure "Alright! Livvy is off the table." Choosing to ignore that, I had just snapped at him about being a gentleman.

The amusement park was only a 15-minute drive. I stepped down off the steps that he thought belonged to me and got in the car, awaiting the long day I assumed we were bound to have.

Chapter Eighteen:
Damon

Well, I can clearly say that this date wasn't off to a great start, I wasn't trying to piss her off, it just happened. It is refreshing that she's playing a little hard to get, that just means that when I get her under me it'll all be worth it in the end. Just thinking about her makes me hard and I have to stop before I can't help myself and give into what she wants. Which clearly, is just my dick, so that she can then move on. I think she is more of a friend with benefits type of person than a relationship girl. She has mentioned this before, but I thought that was just what she wanted me to think, now I'm really starting to believe it. And after the talk with her brother about Tristan and what he did to her I can understand why she's like this. It just means I'll have to put more effort in then normal and I'm okay with that.

"So, I know that I told you where we are going, and I'm hoping that you are okay with it. It is one of my favorite places to go that I can just be relaxed and blend in with everyone else. No one expects a billionaire to go to an amusement park unless they are doing it for publicity. But I just want to be there with you and enjoy this beautiful day." I own a lot of casual clothes, and I love wearing my worn jeans, a t-shirt, and black converse. She looks fantastic too, but she would look great in a tablecloth.

"Are you going to let me pay for anything on this date?" Olivia says back to me, I just caught her checking me out and I quite enjoyed it.

"No, that wouldn't be very gentlemanly of me, would it? I told you that I would double my charity donation and I wasn't kidding, but I wanted this second date with you, so I feel it is only right that I pay. I don't want you to feel like you have to pay for anything when you're with me, I work hard for my money, and I like treating the people I care about. We also don't need to compare me to Chellsea's date from hell."

She stares off out the window of the town car and makes a little hmmp noise. "Fine, but I would like to pay for something."

"Ok, I'll make you a deal. If you enjoy yourself today, then we'll go out again and you can pick what we do and pay for it. But after that I want to be the one to spoil you."

That made her turn around and look at me "You make it sound as though I'm going to agree to start dating you. Whatever gave you that impression?"

I smiled and shrugged "Wishful thinking."

Just then, we arrive. I flash the VIP worker a barcode on my phone, and we are let in. We enter and are surrounded by a gift-shop and some midway games. "Where do you want to start? Are you hungry? Do you want to play some games or start with the rides?"

Chapter Nineteen:
Olivia

He is delusional if he thinks I am going to date him! "Let's start with the rides" That way I can't hear him speak and I can just forget everything for the next hour.

"Let's go on the revelation" I flashed a big smile at him, let's see how he can hold up to that. The ride is considered the most extreme ride in the world. I have never been on, but I am sure I can handle it. Damon looked at me with shock on his face that quickly turned into a little grin and took my hand. "Sounds good to me darling."

Since this is one of the paid rides at the park there was no line. Walking up to it seeing how big it actually was I silently gulped to myself, what have I gotten myself into it? Damon looks over and see's the look on my face, he leans over and whispers in my ear "We don't have to do this if you're scared."

I shook my head "No way, I love thrill rides. Let's go!" The attendants go over the ride, telling us we will experience the same G force as fighter pilots and reach a max speed of 100 Kph. Followed by asking if either of us have any heart conditions. We both shake our heads and were led to the lift to get on the ride.

They strap us into what they were calling the cockpit on a 160-foot arm, it took everything not to grab on to Damon's hand, the ride hasn't started yet, and I was already questioning my life choices. The ride starts to lift us up in the air and upside down, I yelped when we got to the top and despite my best efforts, I grabbed Damon's hand as if it was my lifeline. We reach max speed and I braced myself for death or at the very least for this ride to be over and Damon was laughing! LAUGHING!? How can he be laughing at a time like this? The ride finally comes to a stop, I'm still holding Damon's hand in a death grip.

"You okay Liv?"

I nodded wordlessly.

"Can I have my hand back?"

I quickly let go "Yes of course, sorry" I was slightly embarrassed. He hopped off and helped me down, my legs wobbled hitting solid ground, he wrapped an arm around me to keep my balance and guided me back to the fair way. I think he can make the choices for this date going forward.

We made our way through the other rides; I loved the roller-coaster. We grab a couple drinks and take a walk along the beach front.

"How is this for a second date?" Damon gestured for us to sit down.

I took a sip of my water considering the question "I will admit that this is different than our first date. "

"That's not an answer" He replied.

"Of course, it is, it's just not the one you want" I winked at him.

"You are not one for dates, are you?" He asks.

I sighed "No, not really it's been over 5 years since I have been on a second date."

Damon gasped "5 years?! Why?"

I shrugged "It's just a rule I have in place to protect myself, can't get hurt if it's only one night."

Damon shook his head "That is a sad way to live."

"It is what it is. You can't say much you are an extremely eligible bachelor, and you are photographed with a new woman at every event you go to." I did not like being put in the hot seat, I have my reasons why I don't date so let's see how he likes it.

Damon signed and then responded "Yes, but the woman I choose I won't get attached to me. That's not to say that I sleep with them all, I'm not like that. However, my PA insists that I always have a date for the events so that I don't get hit on when I go. Unfortunately, it ends up with me looking like a player. But over the years I've been seen with the same woman at the events I go to, in hopes of stopping the player rumors floating around."

"Hmm, I'm not sure if I believe that you don't sleep around. I mean you're a man, you have needs do you not? Or are you gay?" I smirk at him. "I think I'd like to play some games now." We head over to the games well he answers me "No, I'm not gay, not that I have anything against it. I just choose not to sleep around, if I have the need to have sex, I have a hand. Otherwise, I would find someone that I actually like and sleep with them. Why do you not believe me when I say I don't sleep around? As I recall I was the one that said I wanted a second date with you while you were fine to have sex on the first date and never see me again."

He had me there. We got to the midway games and there was so many to choose from, did we want to play ski ball, ring toss, whatever that game is where you pick a duck and see if you win. Then I saw it, the one I wanted to play. I always liked playing the games where you are shooting a water gun making your character race the others to see who wins. I raced over to the game, turned around and said, "Can we play this one?"

"Well of course we can, I'm not one to disappoint a lady."

I looked him square in the eye "I beg to differ, you may have thrown your money around on our last date, but you didn't end up giving me the thing I wanted the most and that disappointed me." He left me an opening and I had to tell him that one way or another we were having sex tonight. I didn't think he would be able to say no to me twice, especially after our sexting.

"What are you talking about?" He says.

"Well, I told you I wanted sex didn't I? I wasn't kidding. But you didn't want to, so I ended up having to take care of myself." I sat down in the chair and grabbed my gun, looked through the peep hole to make sure I was lined up and waited for other players to join.

"Oh, well I'm sorry about that. I was just trying to be a gentleman. I'll tell you what, lets make a bet."

He had my attention now "What's on the table?"

"If I win, I get to pick the last ride of the night, if you win you get to pick."

"That's lame. What else do you have?"

"Okay, what do you want the prize to be then?"

"You can keep your lame prize if you want, but if I win were having sex tonight, no matter what!"

"Your on, I like my winnings even if I loose" We shook on it and started the game.

On your marks! Get set! GOOOO!" The person in charge of the game shouts. Me, Damon and the other 3 players all try our best to win. I have a competitive streak, so I really want to win. At the moment I'm just behind him in the game. I can still win, almost there, so close, so close.

"We have a winner! What would you like? You can have anything from the first two rows." He says to Damon.

Damon looks over at me, I'm ashamed to say I'm pouting and have my arms crossed "Well, which stuffy would you like?"

"I don't care, I didn't win, you pick!" I state. He laughs and tells the guy we'll take the otter as a reminder of our first date.

Damon hands me the otter and then says "Ok, were going on the drop zone, and then I'm taking you home." He winks at me.

It may be childish, but I pouted the entire way to the ride, I needed him to get me off and BOB wasn't doing it for me. For whatever reason after that first date Damon got himself stuck in my head and now, I want to see if my imagination lives up to the real thing, or if its better. Maybe it's perhaps because I usually just sleep with men when I want to get off, leave them a note and get on with my life.

We arrived at our last event of the night, this ride was next to the first one we got on, my eyes widened at the 100-foot bungee drop ride.

"We couldn't just have sex, could we? Instead, you want to drop us to our death?"

Damon chuckled "It's completely safe, plus who says I'm not taking you back to my place instead of yours?"

I raised my eyebrows at him, alright all or nothing.

Again, no line to give me a time to get a grip, damn rich people and their money, paying for expensive rides and what not. We got strapped in, the pull cord was on his side, but the attendant advised us that either of us could pull it.

Damon offered me his hand this time and I gladly took it watching the ground getting further away from us. The wind was wiping past my face, but I could see the whole park up here. It was beautiful, as long as I didn't look down.

"What are you waiting for pull the cord?" I tried to snap but my voice shook instead.

Damon grinned at me "Nah, I got you where I want you, now you have to talk to me."

I gasped at him "You brought me on this death trap to talk?"

"Yup and since we are the last riders of the night, I slipped the guy an extra 100$ to let us stay until the cord is pulled."

"You are insane?"

"No, my dear I am not, you however are."

"Me?"

"Yes, this is your first second date in 5 years and you don't like relationships. You are a one-of-a-kind woman who just wants sex? Nothing else."

I made a mistake and looked down, I held Damon's hand tighter.

"So what? I'm only 26, after my last relationship I promised myself to never get hurt again and worked my ass off to get my bachelor's in marketing. I found a career that I love, and I can say I did that on my own without some rich guy's wallet" my voice did not shake this time. I have the right to live my life the way I want to.

"Liv listen to me. No one is saying that you aren't self-made, it's one of the qualities I love about you. You're not a gold digger, you care about your friends, and you even went against your stupid rule to go on this date for charity."

I didn't respond; but he continued.

"You are something special weather you want to admit that or not, you deserve someone who can see your worth. To worship the ground you walk on, and most importantly you deserve love in your life."

I opened my mouth to reply but he stopped me before I could. "You know why I picked the otter for you?"

I shook my head.

"Because otters' mate for life, they find their partners they fall in love, and they stay together for the rest of their lives. A life alone is a life wasted. Even if I don't see you tomorrow let it be a reminder you are not alone."

I was genuinely speechless, men didn't call me out or fight me when I wanted to just fuck and go, maybe Damon is different... Maybe there could be something more? No, I need to get us out of here now.

I kissed him and reached over and pulled the rip cord sending us into a free fall.

I pulled the cord on that last ride so that I could get us out of the park and hopefully back to his place where he would fuck me senseless. I was hoping that he would start something in the car on the way, but no such luck, I even tried running my hand up and down his leg, inching closer to his crotch to persuade him to touch me.

We arrived at his house, finally, of course he would live in the penthouse of a fancy apartment building. We enter the building, and he takes us to a row of elevators, I wait in the middle assuming we are waiting, however he walks into the corner, swipes a card and a door that blends into the wall opens up to show an elevator. To say I'm impressed is an understatement, I've never seen one of those before.

I hear a laugh in front of me "Well, are you going to join me or are you going to stand out there all night long?" Damon smirks at me.

I walk into the elevator, the door closes, I throw my jacket on the floor and I push him up against the wall. He doesn't even miss a beat; it feels like his hands are everywhere all at once and oh man can this man kiss! He slips his tongue into my mouth as the elevator starts to move, then he moves us to the other side so that he is now in the dominate position. He breaks away from my lips for a second "I've wanted to do this since I saw you at the auction!" Then he slams his lips onto mine again, grabs my hands and puts them above my head with one hand while sliding his other hand under my shirt to grab my breast. His moves down and he slides it behind my head, oh the chills that just gave me!

I push him back up against the other side of the elevator and run my hand down his stomach to find his belt, I undo it. Break my lips from his mouth, give him a hard sexy stare and then drop down to my knees bringing his jeans and boxers with me. Not even giving him a second to catch his breath I look down at his cock, it is rock hard and perfect, much bigger than BOB. I'm going to need a bigger vibrator. I wrap a hand around it and bring my mouth down to the tip where I give it a quick lick before sliding it into my mouth. I glance up at him as I proceed to take his length into my mouth, every glorious inch of it, his eyes are glazed over as he lets out a moan and drops his head against the wall. I get about halfway and then slowly start to slide it out to the tip and then go back down farther this time. Picking up speed I start fucking my throat with his cock and look up at him again, he's close, I can feel it. He is looking at me again. Next thing I know he is gliding my mouth off his cock and ripping my shirt off my body, followed by my bra. Then his mouth is on my nipple well his hand palms my breast. I let out a moan, I love that he wants this as much as I do.

My head hits the wall as I faintly hear a ding, neither of us pays whatever that noise was any mind. My hands are in his hair, running my fingers through it. I don't even feel his hand leave my breast and undo my pants. I just feel his fingers on my hips and then my pants are sliding down my body, I'm surprised he didn't rip those off me too.

Never mind I spoke to soon, I feel the ripping of my pants as he fights to get my legs out, so he decided to rip them off my body instead. He must work out a lot, or he just really wants me, I'll take either. His mouth is on mine again, fierce, tongues intwined, everything feels so good! It feels like he has a million hands and tongues, I can feel him everywhere. One hand slides into my panties as he lets out a moan, it's so sexy when a man moans.

"You are dripping for me" he groans what we both already knew would be the case.

There is another rip, I feel a breeze and then my leg is pushed to the side a few inches as he slides a finger into my heat. He trails soft, hungry kisses down my chest before I feel his sweet tongue on my clit. This man knows exactly what he is doing, how could I even begin to imagine what this would feel like.

"Baby you are so wet for me, and you taste amazing!" He then licks my clit again and starts to suck lightly with just enough pleasure that I now cannot contain my moans. I'm so close and he has barely touched me yet. I let out a scream as I cum, I cum hard.

Damon stands up, looks at his fingers, sticks them in his mouth to lick them off, and moans.

"I need you now! Right now!" I whine.

"What if I just want to eat you out and finger you all night?" He says to me well stroking his cock, which I don't miss. I'm staring at it now, getting more turned on by the second. I don't know what it is about watching a man pleasure him self in-front of me but it's a huge turn on.

"Get a condom on and fuck me already. I want to feel you inside me, show me what you can do with it!"

He reaches down and grabs his pants, digging through a pocket to pull out a condom. I have no idea when he took his pants off after I blew him, but I'm grateful he did. He is moving to slow for me, so I grab the condom from him, open it and slide it down his impressive length. Even if we have to force it, all of that is getting inside me.

"Impatient I see" he lets out a little sexy laugh. As he grabs his manhood again, steps closer to me, lifts one of my legs so that its on his arm and lines the tip up. He runs it up and down my center, getting the tip wet well I squirm, damn near panting. He smacks my clit with the tip twice and then he's in me, filling me to the brim and I'm cumming again already. He lifts my other leg once he's inside me, makes sure I'm pressed against the wall and then starts giving it to me hard and fast. With every thrust I bounce up and down on his cock, I don't think I have stopped coming since he entered me. I'm not going to have a voice tomorrow. He leans down a little bit and nibbles my neck. I'm screaming, I'm sure the entire building can hear us at this point, they know what is happening, I'm sure. He slows, going deeper with every thrust as he grunts. Then he stops, still inside me and carries me into his apartment. I forgot we did all that in an elevator, it's a good thing he has a private one or some poor old couple would have ended up with a show, I'm sure.

We enter his apartment to be greeted by the most adorable husky, I bend down to meet him as he barrels toward us. I remember I'm naked and turn red. Of course, the dog doesn't care that I'm naked, so I say hello to him and scratch behind his ears.
"His name is Jack, he's five years old next week." Damon says to me as he walks into the house farther with all of our clothes, or lack there of, I guess.
I stand up and follow him into an elegant kitchen, tidy and clean smelling. I've my kitchen doesn't look this, he must have a good house keeper. Or he's just not home enough to worry about it.

"So, umm... you kind of ripped a lot of my clothes off back there and I'd like to not strut around naked for the rest of the night, so is there anyway I could borrow some clothes from you?"

"Oh, yes of course. Sorry about that, follow me."

"I'm not saying I didn't enjoy it; I'd just like to have some clothes."

He leads me into his bedroom, he has a huge king size bed, it looks very comfortable. What am I saying? It sounds like I'm planning to stay the night, which I'm not. This is sex, dinner, more sex and then I'm out of here. I'll likely make up some excuse about having to leave later, I just have to think of one now.

Damon walks towards me in a pair of boxer briefs holding some clothes. "I wasn't sure if you would prefer sweatpants and a top, or boxers and a top. So, I brought both just in case."

"Thank you" I say as I take the latter option.

I get dressed and then meet him in the kitchen, he is standing in front of the stove turning on a burner.

"Do you have any preferences for supper?" He asks without looking over his shoulder.

"No, whatever you have planned is fine. Do you need any help?"

"Nope, I'm good. I made most of the parts I needed last night so now its just a matter of putting it all together and heating it up."

"Okay, well at least let me get us a glass of wine or something."

"Oh, sure. Go ahead, pick whatever you'd like. Glasses are beside the fridge."

"Do you have a preference on the type? Would one go better with what were having tonight then another?"

"White wine I think would be best. We're having chicken Florentine pasta, it's one of my favorites."

"Oh, that sounds yummy. I've never had that before, what's in it? Are you sure I can't help? I'm a pretty good cook you know."

"If you'd really like to help you are welcome to. It consists of garlic, spinach, pasta, chicken, bacon, and onions. First, we start of by adding some butter to the pan, along with the bacon. Let that cook up a bit and then well move onto the next step. "

I do as he says, he already has the bacon chopped up, so that definitely makes things easier. "Do you have a recipe for this or are you just doing it out of your head?"

"I've made it so many times that I've just remembered it now" he says from behind me.

"Okay next, we're going to add the onions, here you go."

I look back at him, then at the container of red onions he's holding. "You really had this planned out, didn't you?"

"I did, I didn't want you to have to come up with something to eat, or us order in. I wanted to be able to cook for you. My mother once told me that if a guy is to ask a woman out on a date, they better have the whole thing planned because a woman doesn't want to have to come up with things to do. I took it to heart." He lets out a little laugh. "Now we're going to add some garlic and the spinach. You're going to cook that down."

"That's sweet of you. I like this version of the date very much. Your mother is a smart woman."

"You like my laid-back side hey? She is for sure; I can't wait for you to meet her."

"I do, very much so. Okay the spinach is good, now what?" I choose to ignore the comment about meeting his mother, tonight is the night everything ends. I will NOT be meeting any part of his family.

"Now, add this chicken in there, stir a bit and then add in the sauce and cream. Then were going to add in the pasta in a minute. I'm just going to pop it in the microwave quick to help heat it up."

The microwave goes off and we add the noodles in as well. The kitchen smells amazing, and I can't wait to dig in.

"Okay, now we just wait for it to reduce a little bit. In the meantime, we can cut up the garlic bread."

"Garlic bread? When did you have time to do that?"

"I had it in the oven before you came out of the room. I just bought one of those ones from the store, they make it well and I figured why mess with something that's already good? Ill set the table. Stir that once and it should be good to go."

I meet him at the table with our wine glasses just as he brings the pan of pasta in and sets it on the potholder. We dish out some food and clink wine glasses.

"Cheers, To our second date"
"Cheers"
I let out a grown as the food hits my tongue, oh my god. This is literally the best pasta I've ever had, there is so many flavors. I might need to keep him around just to cook for me, I'm sure he has other things up his sleeve. Wait! What am I saying? Sex and done, that's what I do. There's to be none of this relationship talk! No way, no how. Tonight, is the night we say goodbye. I got sex and now its time to move on. Even if he does seem to be a great guy.

We finish up with dinner after some small talk and then bring all the dishes into the kitchen and rinse them off, soaking the pan we used to make the pasta itself and then take our wine into the living room.

"Well, do you want to have a shower? I could go for a shower." Damon asks me.

"That sounds like a great plan. Lead the way." I finish my wine and set my glass down on the table.

He leads me into the bedroom again and we enter the ensuite bathroom, holy smokes, I need this shower! Is this really a shower? He would hate to have to shower at my house after this! What am I thinking? He's never coming to my house so what does it matter?

He turns on the shower, it cascades from the top and the sides, its like a waterfall. I can't wait to get in, I strip down and head in. "Oh, that feels amazing! I never want to leave."

"So, you'll stay for the shower then? Perfect, sounds like a match made in heaven. If you spend all your time in the shower, I can always admire your body."

I turn around and look at him, his abs are glistening with water and his cock is hard. Its pointing at me as if asking me to do something with it. I can think of something Id like to do with it. I grab it in my hand and slowly start to stroke it. Then I kiss him, next thing I know I'm pushed up against the wall and there is a jet shooting water in just the right spot. I let out a moan and wiggle a little bit.

"Are you okay? Do you want me to stop?"

"No, I'm good. There's a jet behind me and its in the perfect spot. I'm sure if you touch me ill be a puddle soon enough."

"Oh, you mean like this?" He brings his hand down between my legs and very lightly touches my clit.

"I'm close. I'm so close" I scream out "please... don't stop. Oh my god, yes!"

His lips meet mine again as he slips a finger into my pussy and rubs his thumb along my clit with just enough pressure. I stop playing with him and look into these eyes "I need you now, please!"

"Fuck!" He looks out of the shower and sees are heap of clothes on the ground "I have to get a condom, they're in my bedroom. Ill be right back. Sorry! Play with yourself until I return."

"Wait! I'm clean and on the pill."

"I'm clean too, are you sure about this? I have no problem going to get a condom."

"I know, that's why I'm okay with it. Please, Damon, I need you!" I whine a little bit, needing to feel his cock buried deep inside me. He doesn't waste a minute. He picks me up, pushes me back against the shower wall and then slides into me. "It feels so good, just stay there for a second. Mmmmm" I say as I press my lips to his again. And then bounce a little to tell him it's okay to trust without stopping the kiss.

He doesn't disappoint in the slightest. I'm cumming again the second he starts move. You know he's doing a good job when this happens ladies, if not, then you might want to train him better. I wish I could keep Damon around just for the sex and the food, but I can't, I promised myself I wouldn't let myself be hurt again. He is also 100% a relationship kind of guy, not a fuck em and dump em guy. He grabs my tit with one hand well his other one holds my ass to keep me from falling. I think we could have sex like this without the wall, I'm sure he's buff enough to hold me as he thrust into me.

"Baby, I'm close! I'm sorry I'm not going to last as long this time but you're my first bareback and you feel amazing."

"It's ok, I've come twice already, and I'm close again. Let go!"

He cums and I feel the pulse of it, I love that feeling. Makes me let go myself.

He gives me another kiss and then we shower, we head into the bedroom and curl up on the bed. Next thing I know I'm asleep, I woke up with his arms around me the sun was starting to rise.

I glance at the clock and its 5am. It's time to go, I've stayed to long already, I can't be here when he wakes up.
I put the clothes he gave me back on, my bra, as well as the sweatpants he offered me before. Then I slip my jacket on, give Jack a pet and leave a note on the pillow beside him.

Thank you for a wonderful night. I had a great time. It was lovely to meet you. -Liv

I searched my purse for my sunglasses and put my hair up in a ponytail. I checked my phone, but my battery was at 2% I silently cursed myself for not bringing a charger I knew better than that. I left his building and walked down the street looking for a café or restaurant to use a phone, it was raining and cold. I found a family run restaurant not far away but by the time I got in the door I was soaked head to toe. The waitress came up to me with a pot of coffee in hand.
"May I use your phone to call a cab please" I smiled
"Oh honey, of course! Would you like some coffee while you wait... on the house" She has seen the walk of shame before I take it.
I called a cab and waited in a booth for the cab to arrive. The waitress brought me a coffee and gave me a sympathetic smile. I smiled back at her; this is why I always bring a charger with me.

When the cab arrived, I left a 20 on the table and said thank you as I left.
I gave the driver my address and silently hopped that the girls wouldn't be up yet.

Chapter Twenty:
Damon

My alarm went off for 5:30, I cursed to myself
that I had forgotten to turn it off. I hope it didn't
wake up Olivia, maybe I can surprise her with
breakfast in bed. I rolled over and to give her a
kiss before heading to the kitchen, but she was
gone. I sat up with a start and scanned the room.
I jumped out of bed as I heard something hit the
floor. I bent over and picked up a piece of
paper.
I read it over again, hoping it would say
something different. We had a perfect night, and
this is how it ends? With a note on the bed? I
sent a text.

Damon
Can we talk about this please...?

I didn't get a reply, she had made it clear she
only wanted sex. What time did she even leave?
I looked out the window, it was raining. I sighed
and made my way to the shower; I may as well
go into work since breakfast in bed is out of the
question.

"Stacy, do you have a moment?" I say loud
enough that she can hear me if she indeed

where she's supposed to be." No answer, ugh. I was hoping this was a false hunch.

I stand up and head towards Erik's office to see the door shut, great! I really don't want to walk in on them but at this point I suppose I have no choice. I knock on the door and turn the handle. This is normal for me and Erik, so he shouldn't be surprised when I walk in, but he is.

I walk in to see Stacy bent over his desk with her hands behind her back and Erik fucking her from behind. How is the office not hearing this right now? They may THINK they're being quite but they're not.

"Erik! Stacy! We need to talk now! Get yourselves presentable and meet me in my office. I will NOT wait" I say as I slam the door and barge back to my office.

Two minutes later Erik and Stacy walk in, she is still straightening her skirt as she sits down looking apologetic. Her lipstick is smudged again, at this point I don't know why she bothers wearing it.

"Erik, get the door. The office doesn't need to hear this." I say to him with a tone that should alert him that I'm pissed off and this will not be taken lightly.

He comes and sits down, "I'm sorry. We were behind the doors of my office so I didn't think it would be a big deal."

"WHAT? How could this NOT be a big deal! This goes against company policy, especially considering you are part owner of the company, and she is MY assistant. I feel that I should be concerned here as well considering you are my identical twin, does this mean that I am to take it that Stacy would like to do this stuff with me as well? Because I will NOT allow that. I have always looked at you as a professional and this is so unprofessional that it hurts."

"What are you saying?" Stacy stammers, I've never heard her so quiet.

"Yes, what are you saying?" He says sternly.

"I'm saying that I am officially now looking for a new assistant. I told you last time this needed to stop Stacy, consider this your notice, you should start looking for another job. I will pay you for the next two weeks, but you will not be welcome back in this office building after the end of the day. If you call downstairs, they might be able to find you a box for all your personal needs. You were a good assistant most days. But I cannot condone whatever this is any further, I wish you the best of luck in the future." I turn my head to Erik "As for you, we will be discussing this in a minute."

Stacy looks over at Erik for help, but him being him doesn't offer her any. She stands up, tears running down her face and walks out the door to pack her things.

"That was harsh little brother" Erik says.

"No! Harsh would have been making you do it. However, she is my assistant, and I couldn't trust that you wouldn't have just used that opportunity for one last fuck on your desk. We've talked about this! You are NOT allowed to fool around with the employees, isn't there enough 'pussy', as your say, out there to fulfil your needs?"

"I liked the convenience of it."

"So that's all she was to you?"

"No, she is a great person. I helped her when I could. But I wasn't going to get serious with her, you know that."

"You cannot fool around with the employees, it can get both of us in trouble, and you should know that. I shouldn't have to tell you. If you keep this up, I'm going to have to buy your shares of the company from you and you will just be considered a regular employee as well. I don't want to do that, but you have my hands tied here. So, smarten up!"

He looks at me astonished "You would do that? To your own brother?"

"Yes, because it shouldn't be so hard to you to keep your dick in your pants. At least at the office, the office needs to come before your dick. Now I know this is a hard concept for you, that's why you're getting a warning for now. Stacy was let go because she hasn't been doing a good job lately and then I walked in on you too not once, but twice. I might never get that sight out of my mind. Thanks for that. You may go. Some of us have work to do."

He gets up and leaves the office. I hope he will take our talk seriously and smarten up. This is not a playground to get his dick wet. It makes me so mad that these two have put me in this position, maybe I was a little harsh on Erik, but I need to kick him in the ass. He needs to learn that just because I let him have 49% shares in my company, I can still take them away from him if I need to. And if he's not going to start taking this company seriously, then I might need to find another right-hand man. Just because he's my brother doesn't mean he doesn't need some hard love once in a while. I'm just hoping this didn't materialize from me being in a bad mood from yesterday morning still. I checked my phone again to see if I had a reply, sadly no word from Olivia.

Chapter Twenty-One:
Olivia

I unlocked my front door and was greeted by the girls all sitting in the living room with coffee.

"Good morning Liv! Looks like you had a good night." Marina raised her mug at me and winked.

"Owe! Owe!! Someone got some last night!" Aly says as she walks to the kitchen to grab me a cup of coffee.

"Now, did you really think you would be able to walk in here at this time and have us not notice that you didn't come home last night? Sit down and tell us about your date." Chellsea says.

"Ugh, you caught me. Okay, okay. It was a great date! We went to the amusement park and then we went back to his house, had supper and then here I am." I rattle off quickly and then take a sip of my coffee. "Mmmmmmmm"

"Nah uh, you know that's not how it works here. Details! D.E.T.A.I.L.S! We want the dets, the GOOD stuff! None of this crap you would tell your parents." Marina says as she rolls her eyes.

"We hooked up, what more do you want me to say?"

"DETAILS" all the girls scream at me.

I sigh. "Fine. So, after the park we went back to his house. Thing is, we didn't even make it to his house before we had sex. You see, he has a personal elevator and its hard to be in a confined space with someone so hot with so much sexual tension. And let me tell you, he knows how to use his equipment!"

Marina gives me the go on gesture.

"He has a dog named Jack, he's the cutest husky ever, super friendly too! So, he made us supper, but he showed me how to make it as well, so that was a cute touch. And then we had shower sex and fell asleep."

"Oh, what did you have for supper?" Chellsea asks.

"You didn't leave the note, did you?" Aly asks with a glare.

"Of course I did." Three sets of eyes glare back at me. "We've reached the end of our journey, this thing was supposed to be over before making it to a second date, but he doubled his donation. You all know this, I don't do relationships, hook ups that's it!"

"Can't you tell that you finally found a good guy here? Don't do this to him, you should have stayed the night and see where it would have went in the morning." Marina says.

"You need to stop with this note business." Aly says.

"Sometimes you have to kiss a few frogs before you find your prince but leaving notes behind is not the way to end things." Chellsea says.

"Whatever, you guys know why I don't do relationships. I'm going to have a shower, I'm a bit sore this morning." I say as I get up, put my mug in the sink and make my way to my room for a shower.

Chapter Twenty-Two:
Damon

I walked into the lobby of Tristan's building, the whole area screamed douche to me, but I am being biased right now since learning about who Tristan really is. I walked to the elevator and made my way to the top floor. The receptionist sitting at her desk was blonde, just like Olivia. For some reason she was consistently looking over her shoulder.

"Mr. Thompson to see Mr. Callaghan" I tried to keep the bitterness out of my tone. I really didn't want to come to this meeting, but Erik made a valid point.

The receptionist blushed and smiled at me "Of course Mr. Thompson, please take a seat I will let Mr. Callaghan know you're here."

I sat down in the waiting area. After a half hour of waiting, I looked over at the receptionist to see why it was taking so long for this meeting, she gave me an apologetic smile. I got up and straightened my jacket getting ready to leave. This was poor business etiquette, making my hate for this man grow more.

"Sorry to keep you waiting champ" a hand came down on my shoulder.

I turned around to see Tristan, blonde hair slicked back and a cheap pinstriped suit. Before I could tell him to shove it, I was leaving he was guiding me towards his office.

"You get how those business meetings can just drone on." He rolled his eyes; this was a piss poor excuse for being late. I knew this tactic that he was pulling to gain the upper hand before negotiations. This alone solidified that I would not be doing business with him at all.

We walked into his office sitting at his oversize desk and plopped his feet on the table. I stayed standing, I did not plan to be here much longer.

"Darren, was it?" he asked.

"Damon but you can call me Mr. Thompson."

"Come on man were going to be working together let's drop the formalities." He gestured for me to take a seat.

I take a seat so that we can be on the same eye level, I'll play this stupid game he's doing just so that I can use it against him. Someone needs to take him down a peg, or several.

"I would like to still treat this as a formal business arrangement. I have not agreed to work with you yet and as of this second I have no desire to."

He looks astonished, not that you can really tell the difference, there is a slight one though.

"What? Why would you say that? I thought that since you agreed to meet with me it was a done deal, and this was just to make sure everything was set in place."

"We haven't agreed on anything, you asked for a meeting, I gave you one. Other than that, you haven't told me anything about what I would be investing in if I agreed to jump on board with you. However, you've disrespected me by making me wait for half an hour before even coming out to see me. Your receptionist didn't even offer me a beverage well I waited, and you still haven't. Then you give me some lame excuse about how business meetings drag on, put your feet up on the desk like were old buddies from high school here to talk about sports. Not to mention your suit is really tacky for the business you do. But please, you've wasted my time already, lets continue, please do tell me your idea."

His mouth hangs open "Excuse me?"

I stand up to leave "Or we can say good day and be on our ways, it's up to you."

I don't think Tristan has ever been talked to like this in his life. He gawked at me for a moment and took his feet off the desk.

"My suit isn't tacky I paid $10,000 for it." He straightened his jacket.

I didn't bother to argue, instead I waited for him to continue.

"It's a simple idea really, my dad mentioned to me that we needed to make us look better in the public eye. So, we're wanting to do a low-income housing project in a new upcoming neighbourhood outside of town."

I was genuinely shocked but tried to not let it show, this is exactly what I have been looking to get into for the next investment project.

"It's a good idea" I admitted.

Tristan grinned; thinking he already got a win.

"Great! I will send the paperwork over to you this afternoon." He held out his hand for me to shake.

I didn't take it "I said it was a good idea, not that I was going to do it with you."

He retracted his hand "Does this have anything to do with Livvy?" he frowned.

"It's Olivia or Liv, you should know that and no it's not. I don't get into business with people who do good things just to look good." I turned to leave his office.

"That fucking bitch" He muttered.

That was the final straw for me, I turned around and grabbed him by the front of his shirt.

"Listen to me! Olivia is certainly not a bitch. After what you did to her, you certainly didn't deserve to have her in your life."

I let go and he stumbles back, he went to open his mouth, but I didn't let him speak.

"Let me make this really clear so you can comprehend this. I will NOT do business with you because you are a slimy snake who needs his father's approval to wipe his own ass. We are done here!"

I walked out of his office. His receptionist was looking at job listings in her area. I figured since I was in the market for a new assistant, I would give her a shot. So, as I was leaving I dropped my business card on her desk.

"I'm currently in the market for a new assistant. Look up my company and see if it's something you would be interested in. If it is, give me a call and we'll set up an interview. If not and he gives you any issues, call my office."

She looked shocked but quickly pocketed my card, and I made my way out of the building.

Chapter Twenty-Three:
Olivia

I sat at my desk looking at the same email for the past hour, try to think of the best response for the next round of advertisements. Chellsea knocked on my door and walked in, I smiled at her.

"You look like you needed a break from your computer. I wanted to see if you wanted to go for lunch."

I stood up and stretched "You know what, lunch sounds great!" I grabbed my purse and jacket and walked out with Chellsea.

We went to the café down the street. It has the best grilled cheese sandwiches and I think that's just what I need to help me get out of my funk. We sat down on the patio with our food and ate while making small talk. I could tell Chellsea wanted to talk about Damon but didn't know how to bring it up.

"Ok, just say what you want to say."

Chellsea snapped up in shock "What?"

"Chels come on, small talk isn't your deal what is it?"

She bit her lower lip. Which is what she always did when she was nervous. "Well, I think you're making a mistake with Damon."

I knew it!

"I just don't date you know this."

"Yes, I get that you have told me the horrible stories about Tristan. But Liv honestly, Damon sounds completely different. I mean, he even sent me a gift basket after my shit show of a date."

I shook my head and took another bite from my sandwich.

"Look, I get it. I tend to romanticize everything; I choose to do it because it's a hell of a lot better than having a salty outlook on every man out there."

"It's just easier that way, I don't want to have to put myself together again."

"First of all, who says you will have to put yourself together again?"

I went to reply but she cut me off.

"Second, and most importantly look at you right now. You are miserable, you can't focus at all, and you're off you game at work."

I gasped at her "I am not off my game at work!"

"Don't bullshit me, you sat at your computer for an hour without writing a memo or anything. I have never seen you so shattered at work since we met."

"Even if that is the case, you proven my point! I am like this because of some guy."

She laughed. "Yeah Liv, some guy that you turned away and because you turned him away you are like this. You did this to yourself not some guy."

I blinked at her, damnit she was right.

"Just give him a real chance. Mar told you to try and you didn't listen, so now I am asking you."

I picked up my phone and looked at the last message Damon had sent me wanting to talk.

"What if I am too late?"

She smiled at me and grabbed my hand. "I highly doubt you're too late, and if you are consider this a lesson." She winked at me.

"Lesson?"

"That it's time to open up again."

I nodded and typed a quick message to Damon.

Olivia

I'm sorry for the radio silence… I'm ready to talk if you want to.

Before I put my phone away my phone buzz's.

Damon

Hey, its okay I'm sure you have been busy. When are you free?

My face broke into a smile. "Guess I'm not too late after all."

Chellsea clapped her hands. "Yay! Tell him to pick you up after work, I'll drive the car home."

I handed her my keys and responded.

Olivia

I'm off work at 6, pick me up?

Damon
I will send a car for you; you can meet me at my office.

Olivia
Sounds good, see you tonight. Xx

It felt strange sending kisses at the end of my message but hey I'm giving it a try.
We finished our lunch and went back to work. Chellsea was right; lunch was exactly what I needed to get out of my funk, even though I wasn't expecting to be called out mid-day. It was the kick I needed. I responded to all my emails, got the new marketing plan sent out to the higher ups and by 5:00 I had already done my work for the day. I rushed to Chellsea's office. "Do you have your cherry red lipstick on you?"
Chellsea waggled her eyebrows at me. "Always, it's in my purse."
"I'm done early, maybe I should just meet him there and surprise him." I quickly touch up my lips.
"Oh! Great idea! I will send Aly a message to pick me up, here take the car." She throws the keys to me.
I catch them and blow her a kiss
"Have fun!" She calls after me.
On the way to the garage, I send Damon a message.

Olivia
Cancel the car, I have mine. I will meet you at your office.

Damon
Car if officially cancelled, can't wait to see you. Let me know when you're on your way and I'll let you know how to get to my office.

I decide to ignore that, this is meant to be a surprise after all. It wouldn't work out that way if I had told him that I was headed there now, would it? No!
Okay it's now or never. I was beside myself; I have spent the last three years shutting myself off from relationships. Being careful not to get feelings; but here I am. Driving to see Damon and tell him that I want to be with him. This is scary, but I am so excited.
I arrive at Damon's building, park on the street. Throwing some quarters in the machine for parking. I adjust my clothes and unbutton the top few buttons of my blouse; and quickly fix my hair. I walk into the building and am met by security.
"Olivia Harper here to see Mr. Thomson please." The security man checks his tablet and nods.
"Top floor room 3487. I will get you access to the elevators." He walks me to the elevator, scans his key card and holds the door as I walked in.
I am practically bouncing in the elevator thinking about how I was going to do this. The top floor opens, and I walk through the hallway feeling as

if I am walking on air. I forgot the number the
guard had given me, I started to read the names
under the numbers. I reached an office labeled
Mr. Thomson; giggling came from behind the
door; I cracked it open to take a peek.
Damon is kissing another girl's neck as he run's
his hand up her leg. She is sitting on his desk. I
drop my cellphone and we make eye contact. I
quickly grab my phone and run back to the
elevator. I press the close button repeatedly; as
the doors finally start closing, I see him running
towards me. Thankfully the doors shut before he
can reach me. I press the button to go back to
the ground floor, my heart was shattered again.

Chapter Twenty-Four:
Damon

My phone buzz's, I'm hoping it's Olivia. I frown when I see it is Erik. What does he want?

Erik
Umm, what does Olivia look like?

What? Why does he care suddenly?

Damon
She is 5'6, blonde, gorgeous, why?

I stand up to go to his office, when I get his response.

Erik
We may have a problem, she just walked in on me and Stacy.

I curse and grab my car keys. I don't even have time to get into Erik in his office with my ex-secretary. What is Stacy even doing here? I told the front desk that she was no longer to be let

into the office! I call Olivia but am sent to
voicemail right away.
I reply to Erik.

Damon
We will be talking when I get back!

I punch in the text, gritting my teeth.
I take the elevator to the garage, continually
trying to call Olivia. Just voicemail, I will have to
go to find her.
"Olivia, please listen to me. That wasn't me that
you saw, I would never do that to you! I promise.
Especially not with what you've been through in
the past. We've worked so hard to get to where
we are now, I wouldn't just throw that away
because of some random girl. You know that you
know me. Please call me!" I hoped I sounded as
desperate as I was.
I decide to try her again to see if she'll pick up
this time. No such luck, I leave her another
voicemail and then text her, all I can do is try.
"Olivia, it was my brother. I have an identical
twin. I'm sorry I didn't tell you, there was a stupid
thing that happened to me back in college where
I was dating this girl, Amanda. I walked in on her
fucking my brother. She wanted to have both of
us, it was like a mission for her, only she didn't
get far because I walked in on her with Erik and
broke things off. Since then, I've refused to tell
people that I am a twin. It is nothing against you,
I don't think you are like that, I don't want you to

ever think I would think that of you. Its just something I've trained myself to do, and I never thought anything of it. Please call me back baby, I want to sort this out. I love you!"

Damon

Olivia, please answer the phone.

That wasn't me, I promise you. I would never do anything like that.

It was my brother. Remember I told you about him?

Please, Olivia.

I'm coming to find you; we need to set this right.

I had just got her to answer me and of course Erik has to go and fuck it up for me. Sometimes I hated having an identical twin, this was a good example of why. Back in college something similar happened. I was dating this girl, Amanda, we were going on 2 weeks, when I walked into my room to see her with my brother. She tried to tell me that she thought it was me, but we both know that's not the case, she wanted to play us both against each other. She wanted him because he was the playboy, the bad boy, all chicks seem to want until they're hurt by them. Surprise, Surprise! She wanted me because I was the sweet one. Guess I got the shit end of the stick there.

I had forgiven Erik back then because he didn't know that we had been seeing each other. We shared a room, so it wasn't a surprise to walk in on him with a woman. But to have it be my woman? That's the part that hurt. Amanda knew that I was a twin, she just wanted to tell people that she was able to get both of us, but I hadn't slept with her yet. I didn't fight to keep her around then; it didn't last long enough to warrant me chasing her.

Olivia, however, is a whole other story. I've fallen for this woman, and I will not give up on her. I will do whatever I need to fix this, I will go on national television and spill my heart if I have to. Whatever it takes to get her back!

I get in my car and drive to her house, she has to go home eventually, right?

Chapter Twenty-Five:
Olivia

I felt so stupid, tears start to sting my eyes. I wipe them away, frustrated that I would allow this to happen again. I don't do commitment; I'm not meant for the happy ever after, fairy tale romance ending in my life.

I rip apart my dresser throwing clothes into my duffle. I need to get away and I need to get away now! There was a soft knock on the door. "Come in!"

I huff as I throw more clothes into my duffle. Marina stands in my doorway "going somewhere?"

She looks at my haphazard packed bag and looks at me with a frown. I stop packing and look up at her, I could no longer hold back everything I was feeling and just let the tears come.

Marina ran over to me wrapping me in a hug, I told her everything that had happened that day. The text's to Damon and going to his office where I saw him kissing another girl. She rubbed my back, but her words of wisdom never came. She handed me the shirt that had not made it into my bag, I put it in and zip up the duffle. She nodded, knowing where I was going.

"How long?"

I sniffled and threw my bag over my shoulder. "Maybe a few days?" I shrugged.

Marina nodded and walked me to my car. "Text me when you're there so I know you made it okay."

I always did, I shut the door and started my car. The cabin was a quite three-hour drive from here. The closer I got the better I started to feel. I turned my volume as loud is it could go to drown out any thoughts of Damon, there is no place for him in my mind anymore.

The thing that hurt me the most with is that I had already said goodbye. I had ended it; I left the note and that was that. But I had been miserable, Chellsea had been right, I had been slacking off at work since then. I used to be able to figure out what I wanted for an event in a week and have it all planned out to the tee with who I had to contact on what day. But I had been working on that particular project for two weeks now and I was maybe halfway through it.

I would have to remember to send an email to work when I got to the cabin telling them I needed to use some of my personal days. I had never asked to use any of them, so it shouldn't be a problem. I had my laptop with me as well, so if something demanding came up, I would be able to work remotely.

I stopped on the side of the road at one of those pit stop areas, I couldn't take it anymore. I was crying and it was getting to the point where I could hardly see. So, I pulled over and cried, I looked at my phone to see a bunch of messages from Damon. So, I threw my phone in the backseat, wiped my eyes and kept driving.

Chapter Twenty-Six:

Damon

I arrived at Olivia's house, walked to her door and knocked. But when it opened, I was greeted by an elderly woman and my face fell.

"Yes? Can I help you?" The lady's voice shook.

"You don't happen to have an Olivia Harper living here, do you?"

"I'm so sorry young man, can you speak up a little, I am hard of hearing."

"Olivia Harper, does she live here?" I said louder and slower for her.

"Oh no, I am sorry my dear there is no Olivia here."

"Sorry to have wasted your time ma'am."

"Oh, don't be silly young man. Come in for a cup of tea, you look like you could use one."

I don't really have time, but I was raised to respect your elders. I can spare twenty minutes for a cup of tea. She leads me into her kitchen where a kettle is already boiling.

"Would you like green or earl grey dear?" She asks.

"Whatever your having is good, thank you."

She walks over with two cups of tea "do you drink it black or with cream and sugar?"

"Black is good, thank you. How have you been?"

"I've been well, thank you young man. I want to hear about this woman your chasing down, Olivia, was it? Tell me about her." She smiles.
A smile lights up my face as well. "Well, I met her at a charity event, she was the organizer for it. Came up with the idea for an auction and I bid on a date with her. I rented out the aquarium, we had supper then walked around and looked at the fish."
"That sounds like a great date, good on you for organizing that. Have you taken her on a second date?"
"I did actually! For the second one we went to the amusement park and then I brought her back to my place and made supper."
"Oh, good men are men that can cook! My husband used to be a phenomenal cook until he couldn't do it anymore. Now our children bring us food occasionally. So, what happened? Why are you looking for her now?"
"Well, you see I am a twin. My brother is the standard playboy you hear about, he works at the office with me. Olivia was supposed to be coming over so that we could have a date when I was done; but instead, she found my brother making out with my ex-assistant. She doesn't know that my brother is my identical twin and thinks it was me, so now she's mad at me."
"Oh dear, you're in a real pickle. How did you end up here though? Don't you know where she lives?"
"I thought I did, because I have picked her up from here before, but I guess she was just using

your address as a scape goat. She seems to be a very secretive person."

"Hmm, well I wish you luck my dear. You feel free to come back whenever you need some grandma time!"

"Thank you, ma'am, I will."

She smiled and said goodbye. When she shut the door, I walked towards my car, I couldn't believe she didn't give me her real address. This has never happened before.

I wasn't giving up and I am not waiting for her to decide if she wanted to message me to hear my side or find out if she listened to any of my voicemails. I started to knock on doors.

I met quite a few characters while on my search for Liv, a cougar who offered to be who I wanted her to be, gross. A six-year-old girl who screamed at me when she opened the door, and a suspicious husband who thought I was fucking his wife. I had to dodge a few fists from that one. As I walked back to my car the bike path caught my eye, I remembered watching Olivia walk through to her 'back yard' of her house on our first date, it must be on the other side.

When I got to the next street over, I saw a beautiful duplex sitting across the street. I remember her telling me how she bought a home big enough for her friends and how they renovated it. I walked up to the door and knocked. This time I was greeted by a young woman around Olivia's age with dark chestnut hair. She looked like she was getting ready for work, her name tag said Marina, I knew I was at the right place.

"Can I help you" she said impatiently.

"Yes, my name is Damon, is Olivia here?"

"She left over an hour ago, you better have a good reason to be here" Marina snarled.

"Can I please come in? I don't know what Liv told you happened but its not true!" I am prepared to beg and whatever else I have to do to win back her trust.

"No, you may not. You can speak from where you are. I'm leaving for work, was just on my way out actually." She says as she grabs her purse, locks the door and heads down the pathway, this is going to be harder than I thought.

"Can you please just tell me where she went? I need to explain that what she thinks she saw isn't what happened."

Marina stops and looks at me with a death glare "you do NOT get to come here and demand that I tell you where she is. If she wanted, you to know she would have told you. Yes, I know what you did, along with our other 2 friends. We were all gunning for you, and you went and fucked that up. So how about you do everyone a favor and get off my property? Go fuck with some other girls' life. Olivia has been hurt too much to be with someone like you."

She turned around and climbed into her car. Now what do I do? Guess I'll come back every day until she either agrees to talk to me or Olivia comes home. For now, I need a stiff drink and my asshole of my brother is buying.

Damon
I'm coming over, you better have a drink ready when I get there.

Erik
Beer or the hard stuff?

Damon
What do you think?

Erik
On it, it'll be waiting for you.

I arrive at my Erik's penthouse in just under 15 minutes.
"Here you go." He says cautiously, walking over to me holding 2 fingers of whiskey. I shoot it and hand it back. He pours me another, I shoot that one as well.
"One more for sipping." He pours one more and I walk over to the couch with it, set it on the table and stare at my brother.
"What?"
"You know what, I'm trying to plot ways of your death. I love you, but I hate you. So, I'm thinking torture is the best of both worlds, because then no one dies."
"I'm sorry, why was Olivia even there?"

"Olivia? You think she's the problem here? No, you are the problem. Not only are you not supposed to be fooling around with the staff, even ex staff, which we've talked about before. But your not supposed to do it in plain sight for sure! Now, you lost me my girlfriend, she wont even talk to me."

"Woah, woah, woah! What? Girlfriend? I thought that because Stacy didn't work there anymore that it wouldn't matter."

"Yes girlfriend, she had finally agreed to go out with me, and then this happened!" I say as I grab my head and put it between my legs. "As for Stacy, it is still NOT okay to be hooking up with her, especially at the office, I should be firing you as well. But I can't because your partner. But we'll need to work something out. Maybe you can be the silent partner and work from home. Or ill do what I said before and buy your shares from you, I have to think about this."

"Hey, I'm good with that. Then I can fuck them instead of just fool around."

My head whips up so fast I might suffer from whip lash. "No, no you cannot! If you sleep with an employee again I will have to buy your shares from you and run it solo. This is NOT the look I want for my company. It's bad enough that we look the same and everyone thinks I'm sleeping around. But now I have a girlfriend and its fully come around. You lost me my girlfriend Erik! You need to grow up!"

"I'm sorry, okay?! You know I like the ladies, and its not my fault that we look the same."

"Your right its not, but it is your fault that you throw yourself at anyone that is stupid enough to spread their legs for you."

"Well why can't you just go explain to Olivia what happened?"

"Oh yeah, good idea! I'll just waltz right up to her and tell her I have a twin brother and he's who she saw. Yeah, I'm sure that'll go over well, considering I've never mentioned that are identical before!"

"Hmmm, that sounds like your fault brother. Why would you hide that? Are you ashamed of me?"

"Of course, I'm not ashamed of you! I just wish you would grow up and see that its not just your life your fucking up. Couldn't you try to settle down with a nice woman? Do you really have to ask me that after Amanda? All she wanted was to hook up with both of us because were twins. I'd like to not repeat that."

"And why would I want to do that? So that I'm like you? Mopey and sad? Amanda was a different breed of woman."

"I'm only like this because of you, you messed this up! This is your fault."

"Ok, so have you tried to see her?"

"I did, she left somewhere, and her friend won't tell me where, said she had to go to work. So, I'm going back there tomorrow to grovel, I'm going to start with her friend and then Olivia, because I don't know where she is unless her friend tells me, or she comes home."

Erik orders in Chinese food, seeing as he can't cook to spare his life and I'm in no position to. Looks like I'll be staying the night.

Chapter Twenty-Seven:
Olivia

I pull up to the cabin and cut the engine, I can
already breathe a little easier. I grabbed my bag
and phone from the back seat and walk to the
front porch. I walk into the cabin and set my
things down. Then I collapse onto the couch and
look around. I needed to dust, I hadn't been here
in about three months after Aly, and I spent
weeks renovating this old beauty to have new
life. I smiled remembering the celebration we
threw when we were done. We all took a week
off work to spend time together out here, hiking,
drinking and so much good food.
My dad always said there was magic within
these walls, no one was allowed to be sad here.
I smiled; thinking about my dad, he was right I
felt better as soon as I drove across the property
line. I got up and grabbed by bag to unpack it. I
looked through my bag and frowned at my
haphazard packing. I definitely wasn't thinking
straight when I was packing and I'm kicking
myself for not already having clothes here. I
closed my drawer and knocked a picture frame
off the top, I bent down to pick it up. It was a
picture of my dad and I the last time we had
come to the cabin. We had hiked to the falls; this
was one of the photos dad had left me in his
letter. I smiled and put it back on my dresser
next to the letter itself, I sighed and picked it up.

My dearest Olivia,
I know my death has come as a surprise, and for that I apologize. I want you to know that I made this decision so that what time we had left was no different. Selfishly I didn't want to see the tears in your eyes, the sadness of the news of my illness would bring to you. Honestly, I didn't want you to remember me as being sick in the end. I want you to remember all the good times, the times that made you smile. Which is why I have left you the cabin, the deed is with my will. The cabin has always been our place, it has been a haven to me before I met your mother, within these walls there holds sanctuary, love and happiness. I hope that for you it will be the same.
Enclosed I had added my favorite pictures of us, to remind you that being your dad has filled my life with so much joy my heart could burst. I will always love you and I wish I was there to see you grow into the amazing women I know you will be. You are the strongest women I know, next to your mother.
From the day we are born we start to die, illness or not we should live everyday like it may be our last. Cherish every moment, take risks and love without boundaries. I want you to be happy Olivia, whatever that looks like to you. I trust you will make good choices. Make sure to keep your brother in line, we all know how he can let his emotions get ahead of him. Most importantly remember that I will always love you.
-Dad

I wiped a tear away, and held the letter to my chest, I wish dad was here now so I could ask his advice or get him to beat up Damon. A heart should always be open, never closed, never locked. That's what he used to tell me, every time I'd sworn to give up on the dating scene. He would always be there to pick up the pieces of my broken heart, from my first crush until Tristan.

Dad had set me up with Tristan to begin with, I think maybe it's because he was sick and wanted to see me happy. I was so concerned about disappointing him that I stayed in a relationship that was toxic. That's not what he would have wanted, so I'm glad things ended when they did. I placed the letter next to the picture on the dresser.

I could always go to Xander as well, he has taken over the roll of dad as well as older brother. He's always there when I need him. I'm just worried about what he would do to Damon if I told him what happened, I don't need him going to jail over this.

Chapter Twenty-Eight:
Damon

I woke up, my head killing me, and my face plastered to the side of Erik's leather couch. I sat up and rubbed the sleep out of my eyes. I feel like hell. I look at my phone, it is already 10am, I slept pass my alarm, or Erik turned it off. I had a voicemail from a number I've never seen before. "Hello, Mr. Thompson this is Audrey from Tristan Callaghan's office. I... I wanted to take you up on your offer about the job, that is if you're still looking for an assistant. Please call me back when you can. Thank you. I hope you have a wonderful day!"

She sounded like she was on the verge of tears. I called the number back, she picked up on the second ring.

"Hello, Mr. Thompson?"

"Good morning, I apologize for missing your call, can you start today?"

"Ye...yes! Oh my god thank you so much sir" she stammered over her words.

"Be at my office in two hours, I will text you the address and let security escort you in."

Erik stumbled into the living room.

"You're going into work now?" He winced at the light, clearly, we both had too much to drink last night. So, I doubt he was the culprit that turned my alarm off.

I nodded "Yes I'm using your shower and one of your suits.".

Coffee in hand I walked into my office, Audrey was sitting there waiting for me, I checked my watch she was a half hour early. This was a good sign.

"They told me to wait in here." She stammered out quickly. Clearly, she was nervous.

I smiled, hoping to set her at ease.

"That's quite alright, shows dedication. Thank you for coming in so quickly."

I sat down and made a call to Erik's assistant, Kyle, to come by in an hour.

"I'm going to have my brother's assistant Kyle come by and train you. I may be taking a couple days off and I need someone to move around appointments on my calendar."

She nodded but didn't say much.

"May I ask why you left?" I asked.

"Mr. Callaghan got really mad after you left, and he tried to take it out on me." She was trying to hold back tears. What had that asshole done to her?

I raised an eyebrow "What do you mean?"

She sniffled. "He cornered me in his office and said I needed to make him feel better otherwise he was going to ruin my career."

I held out the tissue box for her, trying to hide the rage I was feeling.

"He has no control over you here. You are officially hired; I will even double your salary."

She looked up in shock. "You don't have to do that sir, I'm good with the normal rate."

"I insist. No one needs to be treated like that. Are you going to be pressing charges? I think you should, but its up to you."

She sniffled again. "I'm not the first one he has done this to"

"What do you mean?" I was getting angrier with every word.

"Every assistant he's had he... forced himself on them and told them he would deny everything if they talked."

"Do you have any of their numbers?"

She smiled, wiped away her tears and pulled a folder out of her purse. "I was hoping you would ask that" She passed me the folder.

"I will make sure that this gets taken care of. I may need you to make some calls, but I'll let you get settled first."

She nodded. "Thank you again sir."

"No need to thank me. I'm happy to have you here and hope that you will be happy here. I just need you to fill out these forms before you can start." I say as I hand her the packet of forms, I keep on hand for cases like this.

Kyle knocked on the door just as she was finishing up the paperwork. I introduce Kyle to Audrey and give him the run down on what I need him to teach her. Once they were gone, I gave my private investigator a call.

"Trevor here."

"I need you to contact some women and dig up whatever you can on Tristan Callaghan."

He grunted in agreement.

"I will email you all the information that I have."

"I'll get you what I find as soon as possible." We ended the call.

I'm not proud of having a PI but in this business, you never know who you're getting in bed with. I have been using Trevor for the last five years to check into potential investment opportunities. He's saved me more times than I can count.

I'm committing the rest of the day to getting a hold of Olivia. When lunch time hits, I tell Audrey that I might be in tomorrow, but I'm not sure yet. Kyle is free to answer any questions and to have a great night. Then I head back to Olivia's house, Marina answers the door again.

"You again? Don't you know when it's time to give up? She's not home, and she doesn't want to see you." She goes to slam the door in my face, but I stick my foot out.

"Please, just give me a few minutes to explain. Can I please come in and tell you what happened? She has it all wrong."

"I guess so, but this better be good. I only have an hour and a half before I have to get to work. So, make it quick!" Marina says with a frown on her face. But she lets me in and shows me to the kitchen. "One second, your not getting it from just me."

I remember Olivia telling me that she shared the house with all her friends, and I assumed now that that was what Marina is doing, going to get the friends. If this gets me closer to Liv, I'm all for it. At this point I would jump out of a train to be able to see her again, damn Erik putting me into this situation!

"Here you go, you want to gravel? Go ahead, but you're getting the cold shoulder from all of her friends, not just me." Marina says.

"Yeah, I don't know how you could go and hurt our Liv like that! I was gunning for you!" Chellsea says, she looks like she's on the verge of tears.

"I know that you all must have heard that I was apparently cheating on Liv in my office with some chick. But I promise you that wasn't me, it was my twin brother! He's the one that mostly shows up on the internet as well. Please believe me, I love Olivia I wouldn't do something like this!"

Her three friends stare at me with blindsided shock on their faces. "I've never heard that as an excuse before, that a good one, to bad it won't work! You can leave now thanks for stopping in! NOT!" Aly pipes up as she points at the front door.

"I'm telling you the truth, look me up on the internet and my brother comes up. There's got to be a picture of us side by side on there somewhere." I say desperately wanting them to believe me.

"You do realize that the internet can be tampered with, correct? We're not telling you where Liv is, so you may as well just give up well your ahead. Even though your not, but you'll save yourself some time at least." Marina says with her hands on her hips, she's definitely scary when she wants to be.

"Okay, what if I could prove it? I can go and get him. Would that be proof enough to you that I wasn't lying and then you can tell me where she is so I can go get her and explain everything?"

They all look at each other, then back at me and then each other again. "FINE" they all say together. "You have 30 minutes" Marina finishes.

I run out of the house and back to my car, as soon as I start my car, I call my dickhead of a brother.

"Hello, are you calling me to find out where I am so you can caster-ate me? Because I want you to know that its not technically my fault, I didn't know she was going to be here. Plus, I'm not you."

"Just shut up, I'm coming to pick you up and your going to help me fix this."

"Okay, anything. But how do I do that?"

"I'm on my way back to your house and then we're both going to Olivia's house to prove to her friends that your real and that YOU were the douchbag, NOT me! They didn't believe me when I tried to tell them I have a twin so now you're coming with me, because I can't fake you if your beside me."

"Okay, ill meet you downstairs. I'm really sorry!"

"Just please try to keep your dick in your pants, especially around the office!"

I pull up outside his apartment five minutes later. Erik is standing exactly where he said he would be, he really must feel bad. Good!

"So, question, why couldn't you just bring her with you to meet me? Erik asks as I take off towards Liv's house again. Now that I know where she actually lives this is going to be much faster.

"Because she's not at her house, she went home, packed her bags and then took off somewhere. Her friends know where she is but they won't tell me. I remember her telling me about this cabin she loved to go to, but she never told me where it was. I'm assuming that's where she is now."

"Oh, okay that makes sense then. I'm sorry I fucked up your fist real relationship. But I'm here to make it better for you in any way I can."

We arrive at her house, and I knock on the door. Marina answers again "Come in, where is your "Twin"" she says with sass. Just as Erik rounds the corner and steps into the house with me. He follows me to the kitchen.

"I told you I had a twin brother." I look at the girls, their mouths hanging open. They really thought I was lying and that they would never see me again. Well, they thought wrong, I'm going to fight for Olivia no matter what!

"Woah, okay then. Wasn't actually expecting you to be telling the truth, so bonus points for you. However, this doesn't prove that he was the man whore. How do you plan to prove that part" Aly says. That's a good question, how can I prove that?

Erik stands up. "I've put a lot of thought into this, and one thing that is different between the two of us is that I have a dimple when I smile. So, if you go to google and search up our pretty mug you will be able to see who is always with a girl. I'm not sorry to say that I get more ass than my brother. My brother is a settle down type guy, while I just want to have fun." He winks at Chellsea, honestly, can he not keep it in his pants for more than an hour?

She glared back at him "Any guy who just flops it out for any girl who's willing to open her legs must not be able to use it well enough to get her to stick around." His mouth dropped open and tried to stammer out a few words, next thing I know all the girls have their phones out and are googling to confirm what Erik said.

"Okay, so your right, there is a bunch of pictures of one brother with a dimple and all the girls. So, I guess the last way to prove this is that both of you have to prove who has the dimple. So, stand side by side and smile."

We do as they ask, and they are shown that again Erik is telling the truth.

"Okay, so last thing is that Olivia isn't going to believe this either. I mean I can tell you where she is but it's not going to do any good if you can't prove this to her like you proved it to us. So, what's the next option here?"

Chellsea looks at me. "Oh, one second!" She runs out of their shared door and comes back with a piece of paper and a marker. She scribbles something on the paper and then pushes us toward each other again, hands Erik the sign and tells us to say cheese. I look at the sign and smile, it says "I'm a huge man-whore! I'm sorry! "

Marina tells me how to get to Olivia and says she'll forward the picture to her so that she'll hopefully have seen it before I arrive. We head to my house quick to grab an overnight bag and then make my way to my girl. I'm going to win her back if it's the last thing I do. Erik was told he would be watching Jack well I'm away; he better not fuck anything else up.

Chapter Twenty-Nine:
Olivia

I spent the morning out in the forest, I hadn't made it to the falls yet, but I will later this evening after I get some food in me. I walk back into the cabin and took out some stew to defrost. I sent Marina a quick message and collapsed on the couch. I don't remember falling asleep, but when I woke up the sun was set. I groaned as I wiped the sleep from my eyes and picked up my phone. A reply from Marina, five missed calls from Damon and eighteen text messages as well. I scowled and shut my phone off. I walked over to my kitchen to check to see if my dinner was defrosted enough. I surveyed my cupboards and frowned I decided I needed to drive to the small town near by to get some other essentials for the next few days.

When I got back, I had loaded up on ice cream and other things I needed to survive for a few day. I decided tonight I was going to eat my weight in ice cream and watch sappy romance movies. I kept a selection up here for times like this, or for just when I was here and wanted to watch something. This worked even when I was by myself, it was just better when I had mom or girls around.

The next day was quiet, I prepped meals to replace the ones I will use this weekend. My phone stayed silent where I left it last on my counter, I picked it up and turned it on. Notifications filled the screen, missed calls, texts and voicemails. I sighed this was a bad idea. I put the phone back down and decided a hike is what I needed. I opened the front door and stepped out on to the porch only to see Damon getting out of his car. My heart stopped and I froze in place.

Regardless of everything, seeing Damon, I realized how much I missed him. Our eyes locked, those beautiful blue eyes. He threw his keys to the ground with his bag and ran to me. I ran to him as well and jumped into his arms. He held me tight and spun me around, the anger I felt, the betrayal didn't matter in that moment. I just wanted to stay in his arms forever, although it didn't matter in that moment reality was still there, and we needed to talk.

However, I thought to myself that if he managed to find me, he must have graveled to my girls. They knew what he did and why I was mad, they were very protective, so there's no way he would have gotten here without their help. I can't wait to hear what he went through to get here.

Chapter Thirty:
Damon

Olivia smelled amazing wearing the same perfume from our first date. I could stay like this forever.

"We need to talk" she pushed me away. I had been searching for the past two days for her, first trying to find her actual address was a nightmare, and then I was told that she was at her cabin.

I sighed "You don't understand what happened Liv." Her beautiful ocean eyes looked deep into me as though there was nothing, I could say to fix this.

I could strangle my brother for his lifestyle and regardless of the outcome I am going to be giving him hell when I get home. He won't live this down until me and Olivia are back together, and even then, he might not!

"That wasn't me, it was Erik, he texted me after he saw you running off and was unable to catch you." Olivia was silent for a moment.

She led me to the steps of the porch. "I am scared Damon, like really scared about falling in love again".

There was a tremor in her voice. She has mentioned Tristen before, but she has always changed the subject when the Tristan part of her past came up, I needed to be patient.

"He broke my heart left me in pieces and decided to still try to peruse me just for sex." I clenched a fist on my side, Liv is the most perfect woman who deserves the world if I ever see this man again, I am going to knock him out cold. She took a deep breath and exhaled.
"I believe you Damon, you don't need to go into a deep explanation." I was able to breathe a little easier at that, but I could see that she was hurting. I would do anything to take it away from her, to protect her. I wrapped my arm around her and pulled her close and kissed her on the forehead
"Liv, I love you and I will do anything I can to show you, I am not like him."

Chapter Thirty-One:
Olivia

I honestly believed there was no such thing as a happy ending. The girl doesn't meet the one and they don't fade away into the sunset happily ever after. After Tristan, I couldn't allow myself to trust any other man and even though I thought I was fine with it, I have been so alone. I looked at Damon seeing the desperation in his eyes helps me believe that he is telling the truth. My phone buzzed in my pocket.
"I think you should read that." He said.
I pulled out my phone to see a message from Chellsea, I opened it up to see a picture of all my girls along with Damon and I assume Erik holding a sign-up reading 'I'm a huge man-whore, I'm sorry' I smiled and put my phone away.
"Believe me now?" he asked.
Oh, I sure did, I stood on my tip toes and pressed my lips against his and entangled my fingers in his hair. I took him by surprise, but he became in sync with me immediately. Without losing a beat he wrapped his arms around my waist and hoisted me onto him. I wrapped my legs around him and let him carry me into the cabin. His lips only left mine for a moment to ask where the bedroom was in his low husky voice. He laid me down on the bed, I whimpered losing his warmth. He chuckled and took his shirt off

and climbed back on top of me peppering kisses down my neck. I moaned softly as he moves his hand up my shirt. I leaned into his touch, wanting more. I wanted him to rip my clothes off and he is taking his sweet time.

"I need you" I tried to pull him up for a kiss, he grabbed on to my wrists and pinned it to the bed.

"You, my dear are just going to have to wait" He kissed me and moved my hands above my head.

"Now leave them here or I will stop what I'm doing and start over." I bit my lip and nodded. He lifted my shirt and pushed it up to my wrists. Every kiss he left lit my skin on fire. He reached behind me and unclasped my bra discarding it and my shirt that was still at my wrists. This was much different then our first time in the elevator, I was actually going to have clothes when we were done. His lips found my nipple and took it between his teeth. I gasped and moved my hands to grab the back of his head, wanting more. He caught my hand and pinned it above my head.

"Do you want me to stop?" He asked with that sexy smirk of his.

I shook my head "No."

Smiling he brought his attention back to my breasts. I moaned at his touch, every lick and nip I became wetter for him needing his hard cock inside of me. He made his way down to my pants and pulled them off. Running his hand up my leg and between my thighs. I spread my legs for him hoping he would be enticed to finally fuck me again. How I missed that feeling.

Instead, he plunged his fingers into me, I screamed out in pleasure. He pumped his fingers in and out, bringing me to the edge of ecstasy. I could feel the pressure building, I dropped my arms and gripped the blanket.

He leaned closer to me keeping his pace and whispered in my ear "Cum for me."

I exploded. I grabbed the back of his neck crushing his lips onto mine.

"Please, I need you inside of me" I begged.

He pulled away from me, stood up and grabbed a condom from his pocket. I sat up, unbuttoned his jeans and pushed them down. He quickly put it on and had me in another earth-shattering kiss. He slid in, filling me with his cock. I was at the brink of orgasm already; I tilted my head back and moaned. My nails digging into his shoulder as he picked up speed.

"Oh liv, you feel so good" his voice was husky. I could no longer form words or coherent thoughts; he brought me back to the edge.

I screamed out his name and arched my back as he trusted in one last time. We came together and collapsed. He planted a kiss on my forehead and rolled to my side pulling me into his arms. We were silent for a moment catching our breath. I tilted my head up to look at him as he gave me a lazy smile.

"I love you too." I said.

Chapter Thirty-Two:
Damon

We laid in bed for a while, I took in the cabin for the first time since being here. It was well cared for, looks like Olivia and Aly updated this place throughout the years. It had a rustic modern feel, I would love to spend more time with Olivia here.

"I don't really want to go home yet. I want to stay in this little bubble." Olivia said stifling a yawn.

I smiled at her. "We could stay for the weekend; I already had my new assistant move all my appointments till Tuesday next week."

"Oh? Planned on this going in your favor? Pretty presumptuous if you ask me." She joked but I could see her eyes were filled with joy.

"Wishful planning my dear."

I roll over so I'm on top of her and kiss her passionately with an edge. Those are the best kisses, aren't they?

I slide my tongue into her mouth as she starts to get more excited. I grab her breast, letting out a moan as I do. I don't think I'm ever going to get use to sex with her, it feels amazing every time it happens, I can't get enough.

I lightly pinch her nipple as I slide my other hand down her body to feel how wet she is.

"Mmmmm, your so wet for me already babe."

"That's because you know just want to do." She bites down on my neck softly at first and then with a little more aggression. She grips my back well I slide two fingers into her, lets out a moan, the first ones are the ones I like the most. It really sets the mood for how its going to turn out in my opinion.

"Can I feel you inside me please? I want you now." Olivia whines at me, its such a sexy sound.

"Are you sure? I'm content with teasing you for the moment, or however long you'd like."

"I don't want teasing, I want you. Please Damon, please!" She moans as I slide my cock along her opening, continuing to tease her a bit before I enter her. She's so tight, it should hurt, but it just makes it feel even better. Next thing I know I'm balls deep inside her, trusting slowly at first and then picking up momentum. Her moans are glorious, it shows me that I'm doing my job well. She stiffens and grips onto my back as she cums, she cums in a way I've never really witnessed before. I love that it's one other thing to make her different from all the other girls. I can never seem to last long when I'm with her. Don't get me wrong, its not like I'm in and done. I just mean I would like to go longer, but she just feels so good wrapped around me that I can't help it. I'm close now, and she's cum once already, my goal is for one more and then we can have another round later, or a couple.

I pick up the pace, thrusting hard as I feel her start to tighten, she's almost there. I tweak a nipple as I pick up her leg and put it around my shoulder, that manages to set us both over the edge. I collapse on top of her panting, but I don't want to restrict her, so I quickly slide off her and lay beside her. I sit up and reach for the blankets, kiss her temple and snuggle in for us to have a nap.

Chapter Thirty-Three:
Olivia

I wake up before Damon, I looked down at him peacefully sleeping. I kiss his forehead not wanting to wake him up as I sneak out of bed. I grabbed his shirt and slipped it on, threw my hair up into a bun and made my way to the kitchen. I was famished and I'm sure when Damon wakes up, he will be to.

The sun was starting to set as I pulled out my defrosted spaghetti sauce. I put it in a saucepan to warm up and filled a pot of water for the noodles.

"I was happy there wasn't a note on the pillow when I woke up this time." Damon wrapped his arms around my waist and kissed my neck.

"Well, you know where I live now so I didn't see the point." I laughed, turning around to give him a kiss.

"You certainly didn't make it easy that's for sure." He told me the events that took place when he was trying to find my house. I was in tears laughing too hard to hear the whole story, he'll have to tell me again later.

"Why, didn't you give me your real address anyways?" He asks when he finishes telling me the story.

The water was boiling, I sighed and put the noodles in.

Two Years ago

I sat at my small kitchen table looking at homes to buy. I clicked through each listing; nothing had caught my eye yet. Nothing had what I was looking for; I suppose I could always get a contractor and renovate. Or give up on my dream and just get a regular house.
I came across this dingy duplex in a nice area. It definitely needed work, but the price was right. I had enough to make it mine. I sent an email off to my relator along with a request for a good contractor. I choose to celebrate with a glass of wine, I got up and stretched closing my computer when there was a loud knock on the door. I looked at the clock on the stove; it was 2am, who could it be at this hour?
I peeked through the peep hole and rolled my eyes to see a very intoxicated Tristan. I opened the door watching him sway back and forth.
"What do you want Tristan?" I frowned at him, crossing my arms.
"You, Livvvvvvvvvy. Al..always you" He leaned in for a kiss and stumbled into my apartment.
"No, Tristan! I told you I was done, go home and save yourself the embarrassment." Naturally he didn't listen and flopped onto my couch patting the cushion next to him.
"Come on, Livvy my love. My sun the moon and the stars, and what ever else you want to hear. Let me make your world shake." He had a primal look in his eyes.

I pulled out my phone and ordered him a taxi to come pick him up, trying to ignore his obscene comments.

"30 seconds of disappointment will not make my world shake. I ordered you a cab, you can go wait outside." I held the door open for him. He got up, walked towards me and slammed it shut. "You don't get to tell me no Livvy! I said I want you and I mean now." He grabbed on to my arm pulling me into a kiss. I tried to push him away, but he quickly pinned me to the door.

"Stop!" I yelled as he pawed at my body trying to get my shirt off.

"Shut up and just let this happen. I will make you feel so good" His hands slipped into my pj shorts.

I managed to push him off of me and cocked my fist, punching him in the nose.

"I SAID GET THE FUCK OUT!" I screamed.

"You fucking BITCH!" He regained his footing and held his nose "I will make you pay for this!"

I opened the door and pushed him out. "Don't come back here or next time the cops will be involved."

I locked the door and put the chain on, in case he got a key cut from when we were together. Tristan was still yelling in the hallway outside to let him back in as I called Marina and Xander.

"So yeah... that's why I didn't give you my address" I strained the spaghetti and added it to the sauce.

Chapter Thirty-Four:

Damon

I was boiling, this was clearly a pattern for Tristan.

"I am going to ruin him" I swore.

Olivia walked around the island placed her hand on my clenched fist and kissed my cheek. "Don't do anything that will land you in jail now. He's not worth it, I promise."

I relaxed a little, held her hand and kissed her back "Don't worry my love I won't."

She was getting ready to plate our dinners, I excused myself to make a quick phone call.

"Trevor here."

"Hey, did you find anything?"

Trevor blew out a long breath "I hope you're not planning on working with this guy. He's the worst corporate scum I have ever looked into for you or others."

"That doesn't surprise me, and no I will not be doing business with him."

"What would you like me to do with this then?"

"Take him down, bring it to the news. Other investors whatever you can, as long as you have permission from the other women and whoever else."

"That won't be a problem, they all offered to be named to take him down." He chuckled.

"Give him hell Trev."

I hung up and joined Olivia in the kitchen. I sat down and my mouth started watering. I hadn't realized how hungry I was. I took a bite and groaned.

"Is there anything you can't do?"

Olivia smiled "I'm glad you like it, there is way more than that, just wait till you taste my cookies."

I waggled my eyebrows at her, she smacked my arm.

"Not those cookies" She laughed; it was music to my ears.

***

We spent the next couple days at the cabin enjoy each other's time and our new relationship. It was a new thing for both of us. She hadn't been with anyone since Tristan and I hadn't really been with anyone since college, even then, that doesn't count. I ended up putting my work first but that all stopped here, from now on work would come second. I employed people for a reason, if needed I would hire more people, I could afford it. Hell, with me taking Tristan and his company down maybe I could take more of his employees. I'm sure she had a lot of descent people working there, I would talk to Ashley about that when I see her next. He was just too stupid to treat them well, I'll sit back and enjoy the ride for now. I am perfectly content with living in mine and Olivia's bubble for a little longer. But come Tuesday when we head back into town, she'll have the best gift I can give her, besides Tristan's head on a silver platter.

Chapter Thirty-Five:

Olivia

Today was the day we were headed back into town; I had been in contact with the girls and let them know. I was excited to see them again, it felt like weeks, but that was likely only because I was living in my own world filled with Damon. Since we both drove here, we would both have to drive back separately, we had decided we would go to my house for supper. Marina told me she spent all day making my favourites, Damon was sure in for a treat!

When I walked in the house everyone was busy doing something, I was shocked to see Erik there doing chores of all things.
"What is he doing here?" I raised an eyebrow.
"Oh hi, nice to officially meet you." He held out his hand for me to shake.
"I didn't tell you to stop, when you're done sweeping you can clean the gutters." Chellsea snapped at Erik.
He quickly turned around and went back to sweeping the floors. Damon came in behind me and laughed.
"I don't think I have ever seen you do any chores in your life Erik."
"They put me to work ever since you left, they said I couldn't get off too easy...I have been here every day after work." He frowned but I could tell he didn't mind being here.

"That's right and you will be here every day until we have contemplated that you have done enough."

"Anyone mind if I check the news?" Damon asked as he picks up the remote.

"Sure, go ahead" Marina responded.

Damon clicked on the TV.

"Tristan Callaghan is in hot water after recent allegations of sexual harassment has come to light. Three former assistants have come forward and are seeking justice. More are coming forward since new broke out two days ago. Callaghan Investment stocks are dropping dramatically as their companies are pulling out, they don't want to be associated with him if they can help it. Callaghan is currently on bail right now and awaiting trial next week, Stay tuned for more details."

I looked at the TV in shock, I glanced over to Damon who had a smirk on his face.

"Did you have something to do with this?" I walked over to him.

His smile got wider "Well yes and no, turns out Tristan doesn't like to keep his hands to himself. I just happened to allow it to reach the public."

I felt so many emotions all at once, Tristan has been a nightmare to deal with for so long. I was ignorant to think I was the only one.

Chapter Thirty-Six:

Thirty-Six:

Damon

I couldn't think of a better time to tell Olivia that Tristan was being taken down. He is lower than scum and deserves everything that is coming his way. I read an email just before I came inside.

Dear Mr. Thomson,
Thank you for coming forward with the information against Tristan Callaghan. It is unfortunate that he got to so many women, **but at least now it is being dealt with. We are also appreciative that you donated $10,000 to the woman's abuse centre and have agreed to meet with members of his staff to see if they're a good fit for your company.**
Enclosed; I have a list of all the company's he worked with in the past that said I could give you, **their information. I hope you will be able to help each other out.**
Have a great night.
-Kelly.

"So, what happens now?" Olivia looked at me.

"Well starting Tuesday, me and Erik will start contacting the people he had investing with him and taking whoever we can from him. I have also left my number with a great deal of his current employees and told them to contact me if they're looking for work. His assistant, Audrey, has already been hired as my new one, she started just before I left for the cabin. I plan to ask her for names as well." I turn to look at Erik "You will NOT be fooling around with ANY of the staff. Do you understand this?"

"Yes. I'm sorry! How many times do I have to say I'm sorry?"

"Until we say so" Chellsea pipes up. I think she would be a perfect match for him, the kick in the ass he needs. Maybe one day that'll happen when he gets sick of being with someone new every week.

We all settle in to eat supper and enjoy our night together.

***

I say goodbye to Olivia and head home. I didn't want to leave but I know I have so much to catch up on.

When I get home, I see I have a missed call from Mia. I quickly call her back. She answers on the second ring.

"Why hello, how are you tonight? We're you with someone?" She asks as a hello.

"As a matter of fact, I was, I've entered into a relationship with an amazing woman named

Olivia. We spent the weekend at her cabin a few hours away."

"Oh, that's great news! I guess that means our time is up then?" She sounds a little sad.

"Yes, sorry you didn't get more of a notice, but we fell for each other pretty fast."

"That's perfectly okay, I was hoping you would find someone sooner or later. You're a great man and you deserve to be happy."

"Thank you. I hope you find someone soon."

"Me too, me too! Anyways I just wanted to touch base, so I'll talk to you later on."

"Sounds good, have a good sleep"

"You too, goodnight. I can't wait to meet her."

We hang up and I head to bed.

Tomorrow I will start looking for the perfect ring, I'm going to ask Olivia to marry me. She is the end for me, and I want to spend the rest of my life with her.

Epilogue:

Olivia

I never thought I would see the day when I fell for a man. After Tristan, I told myself I was done, and I would never let myself be hurt again. Well, I was, by mistake, so does that still count? I'm choosing to say it doesn't. Damon didn't do anything wrong; the problem was that I thought it was him when it was really Erik.

Its true what they say you know "You can never trust the internet."

I'm not sure what were going to do now though, I want to be with him, whole heartedly. But I don't want to leave my girls, if I left who would share my side of the apartment with Marina? Would they find someone new to fill my spot for morning coffee talk?

I know these things are childish to think about, but my girls are my life. I'm planning to uproot myself to move him with him. Thing is he hasn't even asked me yet so I'm making all these plans myself. Since agreeing to be with him my mind hasn't stopped with the possibilities.

One thing is for certain, I will NOT say yes until I have met the parents and I 100% can tell that they like me. I can't imagine anyone that raised Damon to be the same type of people that had a hand in raising Tristan, but they did raise Erik as well, so maybe?

Now we need to find someone for all of my girls, Xander and Erik.

Hmm... I wonder if we can get any of them to fall for each other. I know Marina is with someone right now, but I don't feel like that is going to stick. She hasn't told Aly and Chellsea, but she told me that she thinks he's cheating on her. I feel sorry for him if he is, you do NOT want to cross us, especially not Marina...

THE END

Do you want more?
Keep your eyes open for the second book in the Soul Sisters Series.

Acknowledgements:

We would like to acknowledge each other for being one another's rock through this process. When one of us would get stuck the other would jump into help and keep the story moving.
We would also like to acknowledge everyone that was there for us though this exciting journey and never putting us down for dreaming!

About KN Marie

KN Marie started because of two best friends that came together one day and decided they wanted to write a book. Turns out both their middle names were Marie, and the name was born.

Nikki has 2 children and 2 cats where as Kaitie has 3 dogs and a cat. They have known each other for many years but got close after Kaitie's little brother passed away from natural causes. They're each other's rocks though thick and thin and wouldn't change a minute of their friendship.

When writing they are in sync with each other the entire way through, and it is a blessing in disguise. If they could give you one bit of advice, they would tell you to live your dream and write smut with your best friend. You don't know what you're missing until you try!

Much love,

-KN Marie.

Made in the USA
Monee, IL
09 September 2021

76933154R00144